UNDER THE WELSH NOT

A novel about the 'Welsh Not'
period in schools in Wales

Under the Welsh Not

*"the cane is what you'll get
for saying one word in Welsh ..."*

Myrddin ap Dafydd
translated from the Welsh by Susan Walton

Gwasg Carreg Gwalch

First published in Welsh, *Pren a Chansen*, 2018
Published in English: 2019
© Myrddin ap Dafydd/Carreg Gwalch 2019
© English translation: Susan Walton

ISBN: 978-1-84527-683-6

Published with the financial support
of the Welsh Book Council

Cover design: Eleri Owen
Cover image: Chris Iliff
Page 3: Maestir School, St Fagans National Museum of History
Page 4: The 'Welsh Not' discovered at Ysgol y Garth, Bangor
courtesy of Storiel Museum and Art Gallery, Bangor

Published by Gwasg Carreg Gwalch,
12 Iard yr Orsaf, Llanrwst, Wales LL26 0EH
tel: 01492 642031
email: books@carreg-gwalch.cymru
website: www.carreg-gwalch.cymru

Printed and published in Wales

This novel has been inspired by the experience of Owen Jones of Llangernyw who was caned for speaking Welsh with his little brother, Robert Ellis, on his first day at Llangernyw National School – 'Ysgol y Llan'; but most of the other events and characters in the story are fictitious.

Maestir School, St Fagans National Museum of History

The 'Welsh Not' discovered at Ysgol y Garth, Bangor

Prologue

Ysgol y Garth, Bangor, July 1902

"Hey, time for a *paned*, Samson. Leave that wood and come over to the corner here for some tea with the lads!"

A gang of builders take a break from a morning's maintenance work in Ysgol y Garth, Bangor. The youth the gang calls 'Samson' has been taking up old, rotten floorboards in one of the classrooms. He's a strong lad and handles the crowbar skilfully as he lifts the Victorian boards, ready to fit new areas of flooring.

It's the summer holidays and, although there are no children in the school, the headmaster is in his office clearing his desk. After twenty-seven years as head of Ysgol y Garth, Llew Tegid is leaving for a job at the university. Back in the classroom, Samson can't quite bring himself to put his tools down.

"Come on, lad. This'll wait, won't it?" shouts Eben, his workmate.

"Just lifting this bit by the teacher's desk," answers Samson. "I won't be a jiffy – it's rotten – look at this hole in it."

The nails make a sharp snapping noise as the plank is lifted up.

"*Dowcs!*" says Samson. "There's something under the floor here."

He feels around between the joists and lifts a dusty piece of wood out of the gloom.

"Look at this, Eben!"

"It's only a bit of wood, Samson. It'll be handy to put under this hot teapot ..."

"No," says Samson, his large hand brushing the dust off it. "There's some lettering on it ... 'W' and 'N'. What d'you think it's doing under this floor?"

"That tea's going cold, Samson ..."

"Let's have a look," calls Idwal Bottom Rung, another of the builders drinking tea in the corner. He's older and slower in his ways than the youngsters, but he's an intelligent man.

Eventually, Samson puts his crowbar down and brings the piece of wood to show it to Idwal.

"I know exactly what this is," says Idwal, turning it to face the lads. "You see the letters here? The 'W' and 'N'? Welsh Not ..."

Just then, Llew Tegid walks into the classroom.

"I've only come to tell you that I must pop to the university for a meeting. I'll be gone about an hour," he says to the workmen. "Everything alright, is it? Got everything you need?"

"Yes, thanks," answers Idwal. "More than enough. We'll have closed that hole in the floor before dinner. Look what we've uncovered under the boards."

Llew Tegid steps towards him, taking the dusty piece of wood.

"*Uffen!*" the headmaster exclaims when he realises what he is holding. Llew comes from the Bala area, and is normally very considerate and good-natured, but when something upsets him, his Penllyn accent surfaces.

"What's the fuss about a bit of wood?" asks Eben.

"You see this hole at the top?" explains Idwal. "The '*sgwlyn*' – the teacher – would put a loop of string through this, and if a child spoke Welsh in school ..."

"... they'd have the Welsh Not put round their neck. I've heard of this," says Samson, "and then they could pass it on to the next child who spoke Welsh."

"And the last one wearing it at the end of the day would get the cane," says Idwal.

"Did you get the cane for wearing a thing like this in the old days, Idwal?" asks Eben.

"Yes, many a time. Over the Menai Bridge in Porthaethwy, that's where my old school was. But it was the same everywhere in those days."

"A cursed thing, lads," says Llew Tegid. "So many children were abused. They were ashamed of speaking Welsh."

"Did you ever put this round the neck of one of your old pupils, Mister?" Eben asks the headmaster.

"Never. Some unknown teacher has done this school a huge favour by throwing the disgusting thing under the floor before I arrived here, thank goodness."

"The hole in the floorboard!" interrupts Samson. "They probably stuffed the piece of wood through the hole by the teacher's desk."

"And no bad thing" says Llew Tegid. "There are big

changes afoot in the world of Welsh education these days."

"What shall I do with it?" asks Idwal. "Chuck it on the bonfire when we burn those old floorboards?"

The headmaster hesitates.

"No," he says. "I'll keep it, if you don't mind. The horrible old ways haven't completely disappeared yet. We need to remember how we were treated. You can't beat a child for speaking Welsh and then expect us to close our eyes to our history."

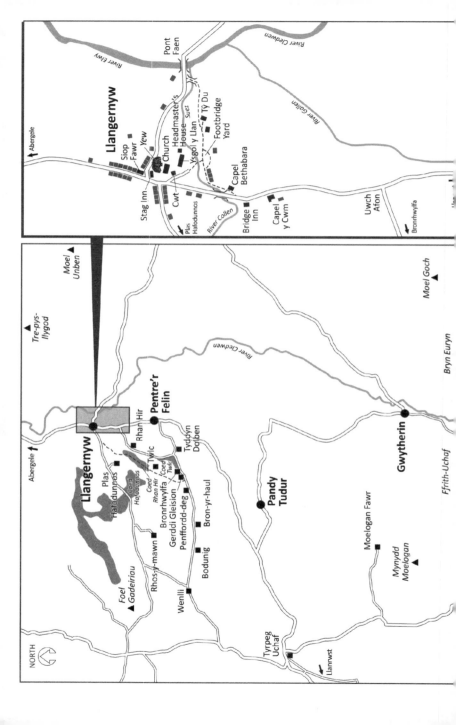

Part 1

Llangernyw, August 1904

Chapter 1

On the last Friday of the school holidays, Owie and I were coming home from the river when we saw Nain Bicycle hurtling towards us. She braked so hard her back wheel sprayed gravel everywhere. "A bat!" she says, with a slight tremor in her voice.

"What's the question, Nain?" asks Owie. Nain Bicycle likes asking questions to try and catch us out. Things like "How is the letter 'A' like a lump of coal? Because it's in the middle of a grate!"

"No, I'm not having you on, Owie. There's a bat in Gerddi Gleision. It's flying round and round and I can't get it to see the door."

"What do you want us to do, Nain?" asks Owie. Gerddi Gleision is the name of Nain's cottage. She lives next door to us, on the other side of a wood called Coed Twlc, above Llangernyw.

"Use this." Nain points at the net in Owie's hand.

"But this is a fishing net, Nain."

"We caught three trout in the Suez, Nain." I can't resist putting in my two penn'orth.

"And Mrs Minister – you know, Mrs Roberts the minister's wife – gave us one-and-six for them. Look!" Owie shows her the shiny coins in his hand.

"Mam will be getting those to help pay for Jac's place in town." Our big brother Jac lodges in a house in Denbigh Street in Llanrwst during the school week.

"You and your Suez, Bob!" says Nain. "Do you actually know where Suez is?"

"Is this a trick question, Nain?" I ask. "The Suez is the straight bit of the river below the churchyard, of course." The Suez is narrow and tranquil in the summer. It is a good place for trout. Owie would go to the far end, where the river narrowed and deepened. He would hold the circular net, which was attached to his stick, in the flow. We would anchor it with stones all round, so the water had to flow through the net. Then I'd go to the lower end, in the Pont Faen direction, and walk up the Suez, splashing with my feet and poking under the banks with my stick. This sends any fish lurking there straight into Owie's net.

"I don't mean that Suez, you lemon!" says Nain, laughing. "Apart from the Suez in Llangernyw, where is the real Suez – do you know?"

"In Egypt, Nain." Owie is ten – two years older than me – so he's handy to have around to answer questions like this. "For ships to go through to the Indian Ocean, isn't it, Nain? Would you like me to list the countries – the British Empire Territories east of Suez – for you?"

"No, you can keep them for when you're back at school next week, my lad. That's stuff for Mr Barnwell the *sgwlyn*. Look at the state of you – you're like two little fishes yourselves!"

Nain Bicycle has only just realised that we are wet from the waist down. That's how it is: you can't get all the trout out of the Suez without getting soaked.

"Do you know what Mrs Minister asked us when we knocked on her front door to see if she wanted fish, Nain?"

"What did she ask, my dear?"

"Are they fresh? And me dripping wet on her front doorstep!"

"And d'you know what Owie said, Nain?" I say, getting my line in. "'Well, how fresh d'you want them, Mrs Roberts?' – They'd only been out of the water two minutes!"

"You weren't cheeky to Mrs Roberts, were you boys?"

"No, Nain."

"No, I'm sure you weren't. You're good lads. Anyway, about this here bat. D'you think you can net it for me, Owie?"

"I can, Nain."

"And I'll chase it towards the net with my stick like I do with the fishes in the Suez, shall I, Nain?"

"Yes, of course, I'll need both of you. Right, let's get a move on."

Nain turns her bike round and pedals back past our house, Bronrhwylfa, towards the cottage of Gerddi Gleision, which is the width of a yard plus a little field further on. Mam joins us at our gate and all four of us arrive at Nain's door together.

"Hadn't you boys better get yourselves dry first?"

"No, there's no time to lose," insists Nain Bicycle. "I don't want that little bat to go and roost in the back of the clock or somewhere and then be flapping round my bed in the middle of the night."

In we go through the low door, into the long cottage. Even on a summer evening like this, it's fairly dark inside. But there's enough light for us to see a black shadow circling the room, fluttering its wings and flying endlessly round and round.

All four of us stand in the doorway, marvelling at its movements for a minute. I've never seen a bat so close before. It opens and closes, opens and closes its wings – but they're not beautiful sharp wings like a swallow's. They look like black canvas stretched along a washing line, with the occasional peg to keep them in place.

The little animal's wings are silent, but there is some sort of high, long 'click' emanating from it every now and again. It sounds scared. It's obvious that it's in a strange place. The poor thing is lost and can't see a way out.

"At it now, Owie!" says Nain Bicycle. "But be careful not to hurt it!"

Owie steps into the room and judges its height with his net. The ceiling is low, so he has to grasp the net's handle low down. He raises it and then there's a 'whap' when the bat comes round the room towards him. But too late. The little black creature flies off ahead of him.

"Try again, Owie!" Nain Bicycle encourages him.

The bat comes past again, but again Owie misses. The bat doesn't look as if it's avoiding the net, just opening and closing its wings and steadily circling.

I go round the other side of the table and start brandishing my stick. But the bat takes no notice of my wild waving and the stick gets nowhere near to hitting it either. This is totally different to fishing in the Suez; the little bat just stays on its own circuit around the kitchen.

Then, suddenly, there is no bat.

"Where did the thing go?" asks Mam.

"I expect it's tired," says Nain. "It must have settled somewhere."

"I think it went towards the window," I say.

As we approach the window, we can see the bat hanging off the curtain.

"Which one of you's man enough to grab it?" asks Nain.

Owie and I are well used to grasping slippery fish and the occasional rabbit, but this thing looks like a mouse that can fly.

"Look how it's closed its wings round itself like a smooth coat," says Mam.

The creature looks too different, too otherworldly to touch. Where would you get hold of it? And yet it's only the size of a three-year-old's fist. And I'm a big boy of seven and a half now!

"The net!" says Nain. "Hold the net up to the curtain here, Owie. Then we'll shake the curtain and it'll drop into it."

Now the net's circular frame is against the curtain. Nain lifts the hem of the curtain and Owie follows her movement. When the net is in place, Nain shakes the back of the curtain to dislodge the bat until it falls into the trap. Owie gathers the top of the net tightly so the bat cannot escape.

"Let's get a proper look at him," says Nain Bicycle.

All four of us examine the creature. He has a nose like a little pig's, just like those we keep in the sty at Bronrhwylfa. There is a sheen like new shoes on his wings, which are more like leather than birds' wings. Tiny little reddish eyes and, compared to the size of its head, enormous ears.

"Ugh, just think if it had got stuck in my hair," Mam says.

"That's an old wives' tale," says Nain.

"It's totally blind, isn't it?" Mam says.

"No, it can see as well as you and me," Nain Bicycle replies. "That's another old wives' tale. But because it hunts at night, its eyes aren't much use to it."

"It can't see where it's going at night, then?" asks Owie.

"Well, it 'sees' by using sound," explains Nain. "It has some sort of squeaky click and it listens to the echo. It can detect a fly twenty yards away without being able to see it."

"But it plainly couldn't see the doorway!" Mam says.

"It's been confused by a strange place, I'd say," says Nain. "Its place is in the woods. Did you see the horseshoe shape at the front of its nose? It's a lesser horseshoe bat, and it can catch up to three thousand midges a night – you know, those tiny flies that bite when the sun's gone down. We'd be eaten alive if it wasn't for the services of this little chap and his family."

"I heard that squeaky click just now," I say.

"I think you're imagining it, Bob," says Mam.

"No, children under ten can hear them," Nain says. "Their ears are sensitive enough."

"Oi! What are you doing with that fishing net? What have you two rascals been up to?"

We hadn't heard him coming along the road. It was Mac, the gamekeeper at the big house. He had come up the footpath past Tyddyn Twlc without us hearing. He's a crosspatch at the best of times. Now he looks as mad as can be – his face is as red as his hair. He has a scarred face with dry skin extending across his left cheek to his ear and round to the back of his neck. When he gets angry, this dry skin turns purple and yellow, making him look terribly ugly and dangerous.

And that is how he is looking now.

Chapter 2

"Now I've caught you, you little poachers! Let me see that fish you've got in that net."

The gamekeeper – Donald MacDonald, to give him his full name – comes through the gate of Gerddi Gleision as if he owns the place. Well, in a manner of speaking you could say he does own the place, because he works for the landowner who lives in Plas Hafodunnos. Mac raises pheasants, destroys foxes and magpies and any other predators – and keeps an eye out for poachers, of course.

He's still yelling, spittle flecking his red beard, but I don't understand a word because all the words are English. Mac's pointing at our wet trousers, and at the net. He suspects we've been in the river – and he's right, of course. The Colonel in the grand house owns the river and every single fish in it. I'm sure this is the lecture Mac is delivering.

This is serious. Mac is pointing at the net and grabbing its handle, which is in Owie's hands. Owie's not letting go.

"No, no, no," says Nain Bicycle "No fishiss – looook!"

"Washing boys in *ffynnon*," Mam chimes in. "Sgool not long off ..."

But Mac continues to rant, his eyes flashing dangerously.

"What's all this shouting about?"

Thank goodness, its Jac and Dad, on their way back from taking a bag of clothes to Jac's digs in town and making arrangements for the new term. Jac can speak good English. He'll put the gamekeeper in his place.

Jac addresses Mac courteously, his head slightly cocked, as if he's asking what on earth all the fuss is about. Mac waves his large, calloused hands and points at Owie and me and the net, his large, bushy eyebrows drawing together threateningly. Then Jac raises his hand and nods his head and says something as if he totally understands the problem, and comes over to Owie and me.

"Tell me the truth, boys, and then it'll be easier for me to lie to him."

"We were selling fish to Mrs Minister," says Owie in a small voice.

"For Mam to have money for you to stay in school," I add.

"What do the little rascals say?" Mac growls, looming threateningly.

"And what have you got in this net?" Jac continues.

Owie shows him the little bat, which is still immobile in its captivity, and bit by bit Jac gets the whole story.

"A heroic deed it was, Jac *bach*," says Nain Bicycle. "These lads have made my life easier. The last thing I want is a cloud of bats in the roof of my house, however good they are at keeping midges away."

"Give this to me," says Jac. He takes the net from Owie's hands, holding it closed with one of his own. He addresses the gamekeeper and I hear the word 'bat'. The keeper repeats the word and then adds 'no fish'? Jac is making a long speech, pointing at the air, at the net and at the road to town. He slaps his forehead and his neck below his ear, as if killing flies, and then points at the trees. Then, like a magician at Abergele fair, he opens his hand and shakes the little bat free.

We all watch the creature open and close its wings and fly away from us until it is just a small, black speck heading for the dark trees.

After a few seconds' silence Mac squares his shoulders, points towards Owie's face and mine, looks us straight in the eye while saying something in a grating tone, and then turns on his heel.

"What did he say, Jac?" I ask, once I can hear the sound of his heavy boots receding down the road.

"He says he wants you two to be beaters next Friday morning, when the grouse shooting on Mynydd Moelogan starts."

"Did he believe your story, Jac?" This is Dad asking; Dad works most of the time on the Colonel's estate farms.

"Yes, I think so. He didn't have much choice after seeing the bat, did he? I said it was a special net for catching bats, bought at Lloyd Jones' shop in town. Hopefully, he won't go there to look for one! I told him that we get a plague of bats here at the end of a summer like this one and that we're busy getting them out of our houses every evening!"

"Good on you, Jac love. It's just as well that you're as much of an Englishman as he is!" says Nain Bicycle.

"Mac's not an Englishman," Dad says. "He's from one of the Scottish islands."

"Well, he doesn't understand Welsh and that's close enough to being English as far as we're concerned," Nain Bicycle says.

"Well, I'm not sure about this business of telling lies, either," says Mam, "I'm really not."

"It was the lesser of two evils, I'm afraid," says Jac, "and it was only a little white lie, after all."

"Right, out of those wet clothes, boys." Mam regains her certainty once more.

"Will the bat come back, Nain?" I ask before leaving.

"No, my dear. They'll live in the trees all summer and then sleep in some cave through the winter. I'm sure that was a young one, one of this year's babies, that had got lost now that it's big enough to go its own way."

"Gosh, maybe that was the first time it had been out of the trees, Nain?" I say.

"Quite possibly, Bob."

"And maybe it thought that home was your house, as it flew in through the open door?"

"Time for you to go home too, Bob, or you'll be making up a long story about a little bat that got lost on its first day out of the wood," says Dad, laughing.

On the way back I ask what this 'beating' is that's happening on Friday. Jac and Owie have been doing it for years, they say. They point at the heather flowering on Mynydd Moelogan. In the heather live the grouse, they say – dozens of them. Friday is something they call the Glorious Twelfth: the twelfth of August. That's the first day the posh people that stay at the Plas – the big house – are allowed to go out onto the mountain to shoot grouse. But because the grouse are clever enough to lurk in the heather, there has to be a row of local lads to walk across the mountain, beating the heather tussocks with their sticks and tramping heavily on the ground, so that the birds rise and fly low towards the guns of the posh people.

"Will you be on Mynydd Moelogan on Friday, Dad?"

"I will, Bob – but not beating. That's a job for little boys."

"Little? I'm not little," Owie insists.

"Do we get paid by them, Dad?"

"Sixpence each for the day, Bob."

"But we get a shilling a day from farmers for weeding turnips," says Owie.

"It's the Master who's asking on Friday – that's different, you see," Dad says. By now we had reached the gate of Bronrhwylfa.

That night, as the last light faded behind the distant mountains, I thought about the bat darting between the trees in the darkness. Squeak and click, picking up the echo. A path of sound in the night. Tree trunks talking to the bat. Beast and branch communicating. I wondered what will happen to the bat when it's ten years old. Will it not be able to hear the squeak, and the return click, by then? Will the trees stop speaking to it? I must remember to ask Nain Bicycle in the morning how come she knows so much about bats.

*   *   *

But when the next morning arrives, I'm being shaken awake by Owie and I hear Mam's voice calling from the kitchen. I rub my eyes and see Owie's shadow dressing as I squint at him.

"Hurry up, Bob."

"Eh?" That's all I can manage.

"Get a move on."

"Are we going to school today?"

"It's Saturday today, you silly billy. Close your mouth – you look like you're catching flies."

I remember about the bat. How nice for it to be able to sleep through the day.

"Owie! Bob! Down here this minute!" It's Mam shouting. I can hear porridge being spooned into bowls. I stretch like a cat and get up. At the window, I see Dad already crossing the yard with a sack in one hand and two sickles in the other.

"Mowing the churchyard!" I say aloud. I remember then. The Reverend Powell, the vicar, had asked Dad to give the grass a cut in the middle of the summer and Owie and I are going to help him.

Chapter 3

"Four thousand years," says Dad.

We are sitting at the base of the huge, old yew in the village churchyard. It's time for our ten o'clock buttermilk and a sandwich and the break is very welcome as the sun is already beating down.

"That's how old they say this tree is," Dad continues. "This is the oldest tree in Wales, so they say."

I'm looking at its trunks. It's as if they're yawning away from each other because of the weight of the dark branches. The bark is red and deeply furrowed.

"Plenty of room for a bat to sleep in one of these nooks," says Owie, pushing his fingers into one of them.

"I wouldn't be surprised if there are plenty of them further up," says Dad.

"So this tree was half the age it is now when Jesus Christ lived on earth?" Owie asks then.

"That head of yours works well, Owie," Dad says. "Yes, you boys think how many things have happened since it started growing."

"It was even here at the time of the Battle of Hastings 1066," Owie says.

"What's that, Dad?" I've never heard those words before.

"Oh, you'll learn stuff like that in that old school soon enough." Dad nods his head to the left. On that side of the churchyard, the other side of the church and below the churchyard wall stands Ysgol y Llan. As we'd cut the grass this morning, we'd glimpsed its steep slate roof through the branches of trees growing on the slope between the churchyard and the school playground. The big house of the *sgwlyn* is on the other side of the school. But there is no sign of Mr Barnwell today.

"You can learn about the kings and queens of England from Edward the First to Victoria too," says Owie. "And to think that this tree is older than all of them."

Owie starts to list them, along with their dates. He closes his eyes, letting a run of names unfurl from his tongue. It isn't Owie speaking, somehow – now my brother seems like just a mouthpiece, open to let the sound out.

"Yes, well," says Dad, rising and stuffing the buttermilk bottle back into his satchel, which hangs from a branch of the yew. "Monday morning will be here soon enough, and you'll get the likes of that when it comes round. Fetch your sickle over here now, to see how to sharpen it properly so there's a good edge on it."

We three go and sit on the churchyard wall. Owie has a pretty good idea how to sharpen because he's been here before to help Dad, but it's my first summer.

"Right, sit like this with the handle of the sickle held firm under your right knee. Hold the blade like this, facing away from you, fingers against the upper side. Grip your sharpening stone in your right hand and work it downwards, like this, until the edge shines. All the way down the half-moon of the blade. Then turn the sickle over and stick the handle under your left knee and do the some thing on the other side. You put a good edge on it, and it'll last you most of the afternoon."

The three of us sharpen for the next ten minutes, Dad sharpening his big scythe and watching we two with our sickles, offering advice now and again. Cutting the last bits round the gravestones and beside the churchyard wall, that's Owie's job and mine, while Dad scythes the wider areas of grass between the rows of graves.

"There we are, these tools should be sharp enough by now," says Dad eventually. "It's a sharp edge, not brawn, that cuts it. Twice as long sharpening, half as long mowing."

Just then we hear the churchyard gate opening. Who should come through it but the vicar. Dad's on his feet, cap in hand.

"Goot mor-ning, Rev-er-unt Powell," he says.

The vicar says something by way of a reply, while looking rather displeased, and then points over his shoulder and says another sentence before heading towards the church door.

"What did he have to say, Dad?" I ask.

"He said sitting on the churchyard wall won't mow the churchyard!" Dad says.

"He must not've heard about sharpening before mowing," says Owie.

"His tongue was sharp enough, though," says Dad. "He said the shooting party is arriving at the Plas this afternoon and then he said they're coming to church tomorrow – and that the Colonel expects the churchyard to be as neat as the Plas lawn by tonight."

We go at it then: cutting, tidying, raking, forking and carrying the cuttings to the pile down the bottom of the churchyard. There are more gravestones than I ever thought possible. I've only been in the churchyard about twice before, walking through to go and listen to something in the church done by the schoolchildren. We didn't bury Taid, Nain Bicycle's husband, in this old churchyard – his grave is down in the new cemetery round the back of the church, within earshot of the river Collen. We don't cut that bit because the posh people don't use the lower gate.

I trace the odd letter with my finger. I can read Welsh quite well, as I'm in Miss Jones' Sunday school class, and because Nain Bicycle brings me books and magazines.

"This word is '*marw*', isn't it, Owie? This gravestone's in Welsh?"

Owie comes over to me and looks at the large, thick gravestone that's fallen from its brick bed onto the path. It's close to the big door of the church and looks rather untidy.

"Yes, '*marw*'. You're right, Bob," Owie says, studying the carved lettering. 'It says '*marw wnaeth*': 'he died', y'see. Well, I should hope so, eh , Bob? Wouldn't be nice if he was here and was still alive, would it?"

"Don't speak ill of the dead, Owie *bach*." Dad has joined us now. He's finished replacing some stones that have worked loose and fallen from the churchyard wall. "This is a gravestone to five children. I knew some of them when I was a lad. Two sisters, three brothers. John, the last one, see – they tried everything, but TB is the disease of the poor; they don't call our cottages 'stone coffins' for nothing, you know."

"This stone is very crooked, isn't it, Dad?" says Owie.

"Well, yes, you're quite right. There's no family left to care for the grave, I wouldn't wonder."

"Is it safe like this?" I ask, squatting over the stone to trace one or two other letters carved into its face.

"Why do these lines stop before they reach the end, Dad?" I ask him, looking at the last four lines of the inscription.

"The names of the children who died, dates and ages – that's the first lines, you see."

I can read 'John', then 'Robert' above him, 'David' above him and then the two girls, 'Margaret' and 'Elizabeth'. Those lines fill the width of the stone.

"Then you have a verse at the end," explained Dad. "Four lines. It's a memorial *englyn*."

"These are all Welsh words, are they, Dad?"

"Yes, Bob. They were a Welsh family."

"So they spoke Welsh in the church then, did they, Dad?"

"Well, there's one service here in Welsh every Sunday, you know."

"But not as many as in the chapel?" I ask.

"No, not as many."

"And no Welsh when the school children come here – like when Owie came here that time?"

"No, there was no Welsh that time, was there." Dad bends over, looking again at the verse and reading it silently to himself. "Hmm, yes – '*marw wnaeth*'. There is nothing we can do sometimes, is there."

Dad straightens his back and sighs.

"Come along," he says, "let's get on and finish. We've not got much to do now. That wall's fine. You boys rake between those two graves there and over there and get your sickles to work on those nettles under the yew branches. I'll lift this gravestone and lay it back flat on its bricks, next to the gravestone of John and Jane Ty'n Ffynnon, their parents. It'll be safer and tidier like that."

Dad goes to the shed on the outside of the churchyard wall, where the hearse is kept, to fetch a pickaxe and crowbar. Owie and I rake and sickle for a while to the pounding sound of the pickaxe. Then we see Dad lifting a corner of the displaced stone with the crowbar. He gets a grip on it, and when he's got a firm grasp of it and is starting to lift it into place he lets the crowbar drop. Goodness, it's a long stone, now you come to look at it properly. Dad has his arms open to full stretch and is bending over with his hands holding its full weight so that it won't fall on its edge and crack. He inches it higher and higher. But its lower end is jammed against his legs now.

On seeing him on his tiptoes, his arms across the width of the stone and leaning forward as far as he can go, Owie has run towards him. "Do you want us to get hold of the bottom end, Dad?"

"No! No!" shouts Dad. "Keep clear. It's terribly heavy. Another inch ... or two ..."

At that, one of Dad's legs gives way and he falls forward.

The stone goes clear over the top of the bed of bricks, but it stays in Dad's arms as he tries to turn it sideways as it goes down. One edge of the heavy stone crushes Dad's hand into the short grass. The other hand has let go of the opposite edge. The stone falls back onto the bricks, but – thank goodness – doesn't break.

One of Dad's hands is a mess of earth and roots and it's already starting to redden with blood. With his other hand he's compressing the small of his back and his face shows he is in pain. It's as if I've been frozen, but Owie is more alert.

"Are you alright, Dad? Can you get up?" Owie supports his shoulders and this time Dad doesn't push him away. I go to help. Between us, we get Dad sitting up and lift the bloodied hand out of the soil. He puts his good hand on the ground and tries to raise himself, but a pain shoots through his body. He gives up.

"Cledwyn Saer," he says, after a moment. "Owie, go and ask him to come here. Bob, you stay with me."

The carpenter's workshop is in the middle of the village and before long the carpenter, his clothes covered in sawdust, is hurrying through the lychgate.

"What's all this, William Jones? What do you want from me – a walking stick or an oak coffin? You've chosen a good spot to lie, fair play to you. We won't need to carry you far."

"I've just twisted my back moving that stone, Cledwyn."

"Let's have a look." He puts one leg behind Dad's back, thrusts his hands under his arms and lifts him onto his feet. Straight away, Dad is doubled-up, leaning forward and breathing deeply in pain.

"The sciatic nerve, William Jones. Lifting too much weight and twisting the backbone at the same time. It'll be bed for you. Come on, we'll do it if we go steady. Lads, get these tools cleared away ..."

Eventually, my arms and legs start moving and doing things, but black thoughts crowd in and give me a headache.

Chapter 4

Next morning, in front of the chapel, people from the area gather round Mam to ask how Dad is. One of them is Mrs Minister – and she gives Owie and me a big wink and says her supper the other night had been very tasty. We've left Dad in bed. If anything, he's worse today: he can't move, let alone get up. The pain has run down his left thigh to his knee; moving his leg is difficult and sitting up, impossible. But he hasn't broken any of his fingers, just mangled and badly bruised them.

Cledwyn Saer had summoned three other men and they had gone back to the churchyard to set the gravestone commemorating the family of five back in its proper place. There was no need, after all, for Reverend Powell to worry that his churchyard wasn't looking tidy for the Plas party. Last night, Owie, Jac and I cleaned out the pigs and the hens, gave them clean water and fed them properly so there was nothing for Dad to fret about.

Before we went into chapel, who turned up out of breath but Ifan my big brother and Betsi my big sister. Both of them are farm servants – Ifan is the youngest farm hand and Betsi is a maid, and they live on the farms where they work. They had heard about the accident and had got permission to visit Dad after the service.

Owie and I went through to the small vestry to Sunday school after the first hymn. Elen Jones is our teacher and she's one of the assistants in Ysgol y Llan as well. It occurs to me that it will be lovely to have a familiar face there when I start school tomorrow.

"Now children, settle down in your places," says Elen Jones kindly. "Before we split into two classes, I want a quick word with those of you who are starting at Ysgol y Llan for the first time tomorrow morning. Put your hands up, you know who you are."

Seven of us raise our hands and Elen Jones counts. Six are five years old and I'm the only seven-year-old who's starting school.

"Right, I want you to realise that Sunday school and Ysgol y Llan are not the same thing and that you must prepare yourselves to behave properly in Ysgol y Llan. Firstly, when you say my name: as you know, I'm Elen Jones here in chapel, but it's Miss Elen in Ysgol y Llan. Say that now, all together: 'Miss Elen'."

"Miss Elen," we seven chant. That wasn't difficult at all.

"But I won't be your teacher. I teach Standard One and Standard Two. And I'm not a teacher like I am in Sunday school, I'm a 'pupil teacher'. Your teacher in the 'infants' – that's the English word for the little children – will be Mrs Barnwell, wife of what you call the *sgwlyn*. But we don't say '*sgwlyn*' in Ysgol y Llan – we say 'headmaster'. And when you speak to Mr Barnwell, you call him 'sir'. Try and remember all that and you'll do very well, I'm sure. And Robat Elis," she says, turning to me, "even though you're old enough to be in my class, you'll be in the infants tomorrow as you, too, are only just starting school."

I'm Bob at home and to my friends, of course, but I'm Robat Elis in chapel.

A six-year-old girl with a mop of curly black hair sitting at the front puts up her hand.

"Yes, Eifiona Jane – do you have a question?"

"So you're an *athrawes* here in Sunday school and a 'teacher' in Ysgol y Llan, yes?"

"That's it, Eifiona Jane. Remembering will come naturally soon enough. I've also got good news for the whole class. The Sunday school with be holding a children's *eisteddfod* here in Capel y Cwm at the beginning of September. There'll be recitation and singing competitions for you and also a handwriting competition. You'll each receive a piece of paper and the task is to write the name 'Capel y Cwm' as tidily as possible on it. There will be three prizes: first, second and third, and a bit of pocket money if you do well. You'll be told about the other competitions next week. But Robat Elis, you'll be competing against children your age in the Eisteddfod y Capel, of course."

Eifiona Jane's hand is in the air again.

"What is it?"

"Will there be pocket money for singing too?"

"Yes – there's pocket money for every competition."

The dark-haired girl smiles happily at her friends. I'd say she was someone who likes singing.

The story of Noah's Ark is what Elen Jones has for us today. I'd heard it before but Elen Jones is a brilliant storyteller and I love listening to her. Noah's Ark is so big ... and we children follow Elen Jones' finger towards the chapel ceiling. And here come the animals two by two – and some of the smallest children actually turn their heads towards the door, expecting to see two monkeys and two elephants. When we get to the part about the ceaseless rain creating the biggest flood the world has ever seen and drowning all the people and all the creatures that hadn't been saved in Noah's Ark, every one of us is very quiet. At the end of the story, Elen Jones asks if anyone has any questions about the lesson.

I venture to raise my hand.

"Yes, Robat Elis?"

"Will you be coming to tell us stories in school too, Elen Jones?"

"Not while you're in the infants' class, Robat Elis, but when you're in Standard One, you'll be getting stories from me then."

"Stories about what, Elen Jones?" I ask.

"Oh, you'll find out then!" she says, laughing affectionately.

A lad with very short hair, sitting to my right, has his hand in the air. Aled is his name and he's only five years old.

"Elen Jones," he starts slowly. "You know the bit in the story of Noah's Ark when you said that all the creatures that weren't in the Ark drowned in the flood, yes ...?"

"Yes, Aled, what about it?"

"Well, did all the fish drown too, or what?"

Some of the class start to giggle. You're never sure with Aled, whether he's saying something to make us laugh or whether his imagination is running away with him.

Elen Jones is laughing too.

"Maybe the fate of the fish was to be caught by Noah to feed the animals in the Ark, Aled!"

"But he only had two worms to go fishing with, Elen Jones!" adds Aled, and then everyone is in stitches.

Another boy who is starting at Ysgol y Llan tomorrow raises his hand. I haven't seen him at Sunday school before.

"Harri!" says Elen Jones. "I'm pleased to welcome you to the Sunday school at the start of this new term. What is your question?"

"Do you tell the story of Noah's Ark at Ysgol y Llan sometimes?"

"Now and again, Harri. Usually every other year."

"And you know when Noah's talking to his sons and telling them that he's had word to build a big boat?" Harri asks.

"Yes, I know. What about it?"

"Well, Noah said that in Welsh to them in Sunday school today, didn't he?"

"Yes, Harri."

"But, in Ysgol y Llan, what language will he tell them in?"

"Oh, the story will be told in English in Ysgol y Llan," says Elen Jones. "It's the English Bible in Ysgol y Llan and the Welsh Bible here, isn't it."

"So Noah's sons speak English too?" asks Harri.

"They understand English in the Ysgol y Llan story, Harri," answers Elen Jones. "There we are, it's time for us to go back through to the chapel for the Benediction now."

"Just one more little thing," Harri persists. "What would happen if Noah spoke English to his sons in the story in Ysgol y Llan but one of his sons forgot where he was and replied in Welsh, thinking he was still in Sunday school?"

"Well, everyone knows what would happen if he did that, don't they?" says Eifiona Jane from the front. "The cane is what you'll get for saying one word in Welsh in Ysgol y Llan."

"I don't need to remind you of that," says Elen Jones. "You know the drill. You won't forget where you are tomorrow, I'm sure of that."

No, we won't forget, I'm sure of that.

But, for all that, I'm not so sure about myself. I'm old to be starting school. I've developed habits. It'll be difficult for me to adapt. Once again, I curse the illness that has cast a shadow over my childhood, keeping me stuck in bed for months at a time and losing me two years of schooling.

After a supper of bread and milk that evening, Nain Bicycle calls in to wish everyone well for the next day.

"I'll be at the door to wave to you when you pass on your way to the County School in Llanrwst, Jac," she says to my oldest brother. "About what time will you go by?"

"Quarter past seven I should think, Nain."

"It's five miles to the school in town, isn't it?" says Nain. "You'll get there by nine, no trouble – it's downhill most of the way. Here, a little something for you to spend in town."

"Oh, there's no need ..." Mam starts to chide.

"It's nothing to do with you!" Nain says sharply. "This is between Jac and me."

"Look at these clever trousers I'm wearing tomorrow – Mam has made them for me." Jac is as tactful as ever.

"They're pretty good, Jac," Nain says. "Your mam has stitched two old, thin pairs together to make one thick pair for the winter. Very clever."

"Does that mean you've got to open two flies when you want to go to the toilet?" asks Owie.

"That's enough, Owie!" says Mam. "Remember, you two – no answering back in Ysgol y Llan tomorrow. What's that English command again, Jac?"

"Don't speak until you are spoken to," replies Jac.

"And what's that in Welsh?" asks Nain Bicycle.

"Shut up til someone tells you to talk," translates Jac, adding "Mr Barnwell the *sgwlyn* and his wife have another saying – 'Little children should be seen and not heard.'"

"And what's the meaning of that in Welsh?" asks Nain Bicycle once more.

"It's a polite way of telling children 'shut up!'"

Chapter 5

Dad hadn't got up by the time that Owie and I left Bronrhwylfa the next morning. We heard him groaning in pain.

Porridge, eaten quietly, and then out the door.

We have about a mile and a half to walk.

The sun has already climbed high above the woods to our left. There's a blue sky and the heat is already intense.

"Come on, we daren't be late," says Owie, when I loiter by a gate to look at Tyddyn Dolben's sheep.

Down we go to the Llanrwst road and then past the pub and along a little path that takes us across a footbridge, right to the school gate. Above us are the churchyard and the church belfry. I feel like I've left one world and landed in another.

"There are three doors, d'you see, Bob?" says Owie as we approach the gate to the school playground. "This is the one for big boys from Standard One upwards; the big girls' one is over there and then the door for the infants – the 'babies' they're called – is that one over there. Understand?"

"Yes, Owie."

"When the bell rings for nine o'clock, the big boys line up beside the boys' door, the girls do the same by their door, and you're supposed to do that, too, beside the infants' door. Got it?"

I don't reply immediately. There is a small man with a grey face beside the gate. He has a long nose and spectacles, and deep furrows down both cheeks as if he's just eaten a lemon. His cheekbones jut out under his eyes. His grey hair is combed flat to his head. He is inclined forward, so his chin is also jutting out. And despite being a small man, it's as if he's looking down his nose at everyone – although some of the older boys are taller and wider than him. He has fierce-looking eyes and his bushy eyebrows form a sort of hedge on his forehead as he frowns at the children arriving at his school. Although I've only seen him maybe twice before in the village, I have no doubt this is Mr Barnwell, the *sgwlyn*.

The most scary thing about him is the yellow cane in his right hand.

Owie is still speaking, telling me the school rules. We go through the gate, past the headmaster and into the playground.

"You understand the lining up thing now, Bob? The most important thing though – don't talk to your friends in class. Oh, and remember to sit still ..."

"Boy!"

If someone had fired a gun next to my ear, I wouldn't have jumped as badly.

Owie jumped too. We both turn to face what is behind us. The man's grey face was white by now, his mouth a hateful, straight line across his face and he's working his two rows of teeth against each other. If anything, he is inclined even further forward and his chin is right in our faces.

He barks a question in Owie's direction.

"Spee-kin' to my bru-ther, sir." Owie replies, his voice tiny, almost inaudible.

The grey man roars and points to the playground and to the school gate. I don't know what the next shout says, but I see Owie extend his right arm and open his hand, palm up.

Whap!

The small, grey man had suddenly straightened and lifted the cane above his head and brought it down with his whole strength on Owie's hand. Then he shouts something else. I can see Owie's eyes filling and his lip trembling. But he pulls back his right arm and extends his left, opens his hand, palm up ...

Whap!

The cane whistles again, and this time I can see the red weal rising on my brother's hand from the blow. The headmaster steps smartly behind Owie and delivers another blow with the cane to his right shoulder, then his left shoulder and then two blows lower down across the backs of his legs until poor Owie is hopping about and his sobbing fills the playground.

All the children are in the playground, standing round us in a semicircle. Everyone is quiet, staring at the scene.

"Six of the best for speaking Welsh!" shouts the headmaster and turned to point the tip of his cane past the row of children. "Now, go to your lines."

Owie is still howling. He's doubled over, with his hands pressed into his armpits. I can see red welts across the backs of his legs. Slowly, he walks towards the line in front of the big boys' door.

I'm gasping and I'm afraid that I'm going to start crying too. The headmaster pushes his chin closer to me.

He growls one harsh word in my face.

I frantically turn my head. But I don't see anyone I know. My shoulders are heaving. Where did Owie say the infants were to line up? And is that where I'm to go? Is Elen Jones, no, Miss Elen about ...? Where ...?

Just then I feel someone grasp my arm. I snap my head round in case there's someone else in the school with a cane. But no, it's a little girl. The little girl with dark curls that was in Sunday school yesterday. Without looking at me and without uttering a work, she leads me by my arm across the playground.

These must be the infants. Yes, I see Aled's head, with his cropped hair like a hedgehog's bristles. He gives me a tiny smile. But no one says a word.

In front of us now there's a heavily built woman. She, too, has grey hair and spectacles. I'm sure she's looking down her nose at us as well. I've no doubt this is Mrs Barnwell, the schoolmaster's wife and the infants' teacher – and mine.

I turn my head to see if Owie is any better by now, but the lines of big lads are walking into school, and the *sgwlyn* is beating his cane on the doorstep as if they're soldiers in the army.

Someone is shouting in my ear.

I turn my head and Mrs Barnwell's face is there in front of me, shouting something. I don't know if it's a question or not, so I study her face.

Her large cheeks make her eyes look small. Similar to a

bat's eyes, I think. But then again her mouth is open and wet – it looks like that of a trout, fished out of the river Collen, I think then. She's harrumphing and turning back towards the infants' door.

"In!" she shouts.

The ones at the head of the queue start to walk into the school and when it's my turn, I follow them.

Inside the school there is one large room. At the far end are the older children and in front of them is the headmaster's high desk, with about six canes on the desk's shelf. Each class has long desks that hold five or six children.

I can see Owie now at the back of the second block of desks, and I try and catch his eye to raise his spirits. In front of the rows of desks closest to those of the infants stands Elen Jones. Our eyes meet for half a second, but then she looks away.

Mrs Barnwell is shouting 'Go something, something'. It sounds as if she's saying '*Go drapiau ulw las!*' but I can't see why would she be saying 'Oh, drat it all!' I'm still between the door out to the playground and the infants' desks.

She comes a step closer and that 'Go' comes out of her mouth again as a scream once more.

This time I get a punch in the back such that I have to put my hands out towards one of the long desks to save myself. Then there's a knee against my leg and I haul myself the length of he desk right to the far end. As I sit, I see that it's Aled who's nudged me to my seat. I say nothing to him, just give him a quick nod.

Mrs Barnwell is saying something else to us now, and

then she goes to sit behind a small desk in front of us. Each of the other teachers is behind their own desk and there is a large book and a pen in the hands of every one of them. They are shouting names and then children's voices are shouting something like 'Heersur' or 'Earmis' from their seats.

Mrs Barnwell starts to shout names now. I notice that they're girls' names and 'Earmis' is what the class says.

"Eifiona Jane Edwards?"

"Earmis."

She's sitting directly in front of me. Is this one of those things that Jac said last night – 'Don't speak until you are spoken to'? Maybe I should start to practise saying 'Earmis' like everyone else? I open my lips to start making the right shape with my mouth but I can't get them to move. It's exactly as if that same miserable illness is back, knotting my windpipe.

Mrs Barnwell has started calling the boys' names now. That very minute Aled, sitting next to me, says 'Earmis' clearly. But my lips don't move and my throat is dry.

"Roburrt Elees Jowns?"

The first thing that goes through my head is that there's someone here with a name similar to mine. I'm Bob to everyone, although 'Robat Elis' in chapel.

"Roburrt Elees Jowns?"

It must be me she means! I open my mouth wider, but my lips don't move. The word feels heavy, and stuck in the bottom of my stomach.

"ROBURRT ELEES JOWNS?"

"Earmis."

And she calls the next name. But it was not me who answered her. And neither had Aled said a word. Suddenly, for a split second only, while Mrs Barnwell is looking across to the far end of the long desk, Eifiona's head of dark curls turns towards me and looks at me without a smile or frown. But only for a split second. But I know then that she had answered on my behalf.

Before long, calling the names and their answering is over. One or two other names had not been responded to either and Mrs Barnwell is cross as she looks about for those names.

Then a tall boy from the village comes in through the big boys' door, his face red from running. He's late.

Mr Barnwell grabs of one of the canes from the shelf on his desk, seizes the boy, and whacks both his hands.

Chapter 6

There isn't a squeak out of anyone as the tall boy makes his
way to sit at one of the further desks. All eyes are now on the
headmaster. He is walking up and down the front of all the
classes holding a length of cord above his head with his left
hand and a cane in his right. There is a piece of wood tied to
the cord. As he comes level with our class, I can read two
letters ...a saw's edge: 'W', then two fenceposts and a
straining post: 'N'.

W.N.

"Something, something ... Welsh Not" Mr Barnwell is
shouting, while simultaneously waving the cane. He's using
the tip of the cane to point at each class in turn and shout
some more. Behind him Elen Jones – Miss Elen – looks at the
floor while he roars at her class.

"Now lettuce pray," he says at the end of the shouting.

I glance over to Owie, wondering why the schoolmaster's
talking about lettuce, and am surprised to see the children in
the other classes on their feet, their heads bowed, their eyes
closed and their hands together. They are praying. The voices
of about seventy children start to chant together. It sounds
like the train as it comes through the Conwy Valley, as heard
from Tyrpeg Uchaf – but the train's in the same room as me.

Mrs Barnwell indicates with her arms for us to stand up. I
half turn as I stand up, and see that the infants that have

already been in school a while are on their feet like everyone else and are reciting the prayer. How on earth do they know all this? I'll never learn all this.

By the time the new infants have all stood up, put their hands together and closed their eyes and bowed their heads, it's over – one 'Amen', the same as in chapel, and the whole school sits down.

Mrs Barnwell is now writing on the board with chalk. I can see that the first thing is a letter – a circle, like an open mouth: the letter 'O'. But a shape like a kiss is the next thing on the blackboard: 'X'.

She makes her mouth round and points at the letter 'O' and then makes the sound 'O'. Then she points at the kiss shape and makes some sort of noise in her throat like the one Dad makes when he's chasing Fly, our dog, away from the hens: 'Css!'

"O," she says again, and "Css!"

She indicates for our class to all stand and it's plain she wants us to make the same noise as her. She points at the 'O' and then points at us.

I make my mouth round. The whole class says 'O' together. But nothing except air comes out of my mouth.

Once more and louder is what I think Mrs Barnwell is signalling now.

The infants all say 'O' but my throat has closed even though my mouth is open.

Again and louder still, say Mrs Barnwell's gesticulations.

The class roars out 'O'. I cannot make the slightest sound. I am truly trying my best. I pull my stomach in. I strain my throat. I'm sure my face is bright red. But not the slightest sound comes out of my mouth.

We remain on our feet. It's the kiss that gets Mrs Barnwell's attention now. She makes that chasing-the-dog-away sound. Twice. Then she turns towards us. 'Css!' everyone says. Except me. I see Fly. I see her prowling round two hens pecking at the farmyard at home. I try my best to shout 'Css!' at Fly, but utter no sound.

Mrs Barwell is making the shape of a bridge with her hand between the letter 'O' and the kiss on the blackboard. With her mouth round to start with and then turning it into a slot like a letterbox , she links the sound 'O' and the 'Css!' together: 'Ocss!'

She points at the class, which is still on its feet.

"Ocss!" says everyone except me.

The mouth is working all right – I start with a round mouth and end with a letterbox. But it's a wholly mute mouth. I can't understand why.

After shouting this three times, we are all allowed to sit down again. I recognise and know the sound of every letter in the chapel Sunday school but I've never in my life seen a 'kiss' as a letter before. I've grasped by now that it's a letter. Some of the Ysgol y Llan letters must be different to Sunday school letters.

Mrs Barnwell has gone to the end nearest the door of each row of infants. She's pointing at those sitting right at the end and is saying something. I see that the little children who have been here before the summer understand what she's saying and they stand and go to the large, brown cupboard behind the door. Mrs Barnwell points at two in the row of those who started for the first time today, and says something sharply to them. They stand and do the same thing as the other little ones.

I see the door of the large, brown cupboard being opened. The door reaches from the floor almost to the ceiling. There are a lot of shelves inside and the row-end children are bending down to the bottom shelves and carrying about half a dozen wooden frames each. I've seen things like this before – we use them in Sunday school. Held in place by the frame is a slate, which can be written upon with a slate pencil.

The writing slates are carried to the ends of the rows and then passed along one by one. The children doing the fetching are then ordered by Mrs Barnwell to bring slate pencils to each row.

By now Mrs Barnwell is standing under a colourful poster in the corner. I instantly recognise a horse, dog, cat, pig, hen, sheep and lamb on the poster. Mrs Barnwell is pointing at a big cow with enormous horns. This isn't a milking cow, but neither is it a bull – it's some sort of a bullock, but with broad and strong shoulders and these huge horns on its head.

Mrs Barnwell is pointing at the horned cow and saying "Ocss!" It's an ocss, then. I've never seen such a creature. It must be what they have in England. She wants us to say the name. Three times. And I fail to say it once.

She says something else and I hear a terrible scratching sound behind me. I take a glance and see a girl with her hair in a plait down her back scraping something on the slate. She's drawing the 'O' and the 'kiss'. A glimpse then of the rest of those behind me and each one has their head bent and their tongue out. What a scraping, scratching noise.

I nudge Aled with my elbow and nod at my slate. I grip the slate pencil and draw the 'O'. That is to say, I'm writing. It's hard to get the start and finish of the 'O' to meet tidily but it's not too bad. I'm used to writing in chapel and at the kitchen table, but scraping letters on slate is a different matter. My 'O' looks a bit like an apple with a lump on it. Then two gate cross-bars – the 'Css!' sound at Fly.

Aled has seen what I'm doing and I hear him trying to do the same thing. Neither of us dares to whisper one word. We all know about the Welsh Not and have seen what the result is if you don't stick to that rule.

The scraping sound has stopped. Mrs Barnwell is shouting something and the scraping starts again behind me. Another quick glance and I see that every child is making more pictures of these letters, one under the other, until they've filled the slate. After doing a couple, this comes easily to me.

After I've got to the bottom of my slate, I lift my head to look at the horned cow again. Yes, she looks like a very strong cow – but she still looks strange. I think about Llanrwst Show. There are all sorts of cattle at the show, not just small black ones with horns, and the odd white-headed one like the ones we have on the hills. I saw brown ones, brown and white, and grey-blue and white in that show. And one with a woolly coat and long horns, too. But I never saw this 'ox' there.

The others are still scratching away at their slates around me and my eyes roam around, looking at other things on the walls. Some rows of figures – 1, 2, 3 and so on – are on the card closest to the animals. A poster of letters then – I know most of them but there are a few that are strange to me there too. What on earth is that one like the back of a stable door at the end? It's made up all of straight lines and it'd be easy to draw, but I've never seen the back of a stable door on paper before: 'Z'.

My eyes wander towards Elen Jones – Miss Elen – in front of the class nearest to us. There are no walls between the classes as there are between the small vestry and the large vestry in the Sunday school, just a sort of aisle between the long desks. Miss Elen has a piece of paper on the wall, also with figures on, and she's pointing at some of them and saying the names of a line of them to the class, and the class then imitates her.

"Wahoaoi!" Mrs Barnwell has just shouted something terrifying in my ear and she looks as cross as a cat that has just been kicked out of the house.

She leans over my desk and snatches up my slate. Then she quietens and she's even making a noise with her mouth that's like the sound I make when I'm eating sweets at the fair – 'mm!' She holds my slate up to the class and points at the two lowest 'O's on it – these are the two roundest letters. The two 'X's nearest them aren't too bad either – the tops and bottoms are more or less level.

Mrs Barnwell says something in a softer voice and there is the almost a smile on her face as she returns my slate to me. She says something that sounds like a question and waits for an answer.

I'm on the point of thanking her by saying '*Diolch yn fawr*' but then remember in time about the Welsh Not. I do nothing except nod my head up and down like a cow licking her calf. But she's still asking some question that sound like 'Eor-naym'.

It dawns on me then that she wants me to say the word.

"Eor-naym!" she demands, and the hint of the smile under her nose has disappeared.

I make my mouth round and I look as if I'm about to say something ... but I know no sound will come out of my mouth.

That's when one of the big lads rings the bell beside the big lads' door.

"Robat, miss." I hear this before the last clang of the bell fades.

That wasn't my voice but someone has said my name.

Mrs Barnwell walks past me now and says something that includes my name. Except that she calls me 'Roburrt'.

But it's playtime now. I know what that bell means. We can go out into the sunshine now.

Chapter 7

When we get back to our desks, a big lass with fair hair is crying in the headmaster's class. Mrs Barnwell is standing at her husband's side and pointing at her, and accusing her. After she's done, Mrs Barnwell comes back to stand in front of our class but everyone's eyes are on the headmaster now.

He reaches for the Welsh Not that's hanging from a peg on his class' blackboard and carries it forward with both hands. He's saying something about 'Welsh' and 'Gillian Davies' and his voice rises to a screech at the end.

Gillian Davies – that's the blonde girl's name, I take it – is sobbing now, the tears rolling down her flushed cheeks. She has bent her head so low that her nose is almost touching the desk and has retreated into herself.

A little time earlier Gillian and her friend were playing in the playground. The playground is divided into two parts: the girls and the infants – including me – at one end and the big boys at the other. We infants hadn't done much during playtime, only stood by the wall and watched the big girls playing. They were skipping with a long rope, counting as the rope whipped over them and dropping out to make way for someone else if they mis-stepped and the rope hit their legs.

Gillian was having a good run at skipping but one of the girls holding the end of the rope let go suddenly and Gillian had to stop. An argument ensued as to whether Gillian was 'out' or not.

"It's not my fault that fool let go of the rope, is it?" shouted Gillian in Welsh.

She'd got back to skipping in the end, but I see Harri, the shopkeeper's son, leave our wall and go to say something to Mrs Barnwell, who was standing on the doorstep. I saw her nod and fold her arms.

I had no doubt that it was Harri who had snitched on Gillian for speaking Welsh at playtime. Now she was having to straighten up as Mr Barnwell shouted at her, and lift her head as he placed the cord round her neck and let the wooden board with the 'W.N.' hang down her front.

The headmaster goes back to his desk and raises a cane and he's ranting about something. He finishes by whacking his desk lid hard with his cane. Gillian starts blubbering again.

I turn to look at Harri, sitting further down the front row from me. It was almost as if there were a sly smirk on his face by now. All of us knew, even before we started school, what the rule was. Because he'd told on another child, if he were to be caught speaking Welsh in the future, he'd be let off the first time with a warning. If he were to be caught a second time, he'd get the Welsh Not like everyone else, of course. But he had one chance in the bank now.

The onus was now on Gillian. If she were to hear someone say just one word of Welsh, she could report them and be rid of the Welsh Not. If she didn't hear any Welsh from anyone – or if she didn't tell – she would get the cane at the end of the afternoon.

Very quietly, every class went back to work for the rest of the morning. Mrs Barnwell had moved to the card with figures on now. Pointing at the figures, she says the name and then we all stand up and recite the name of the number in unison. Once again, I try to make the right shapes with my mouth but my throat has closed up. By dinner time we are scratching the first three numbers over and over on our slates. I know them – they're *un*, *dau*, *tri* in Sunday school, but I can't say what they are in Ysgol y Llan.

Out in the playground, Gillian's not playing with the skipping rope gang this time. She is shunned. When she gets close to anyone, that child walks away. The piece of wood bangs her chest awkwardly as she walks, and she constantly fidgets with the cord round her neck because it's chafing her skin. She gets closer to the boys' side every so often but they understand the situation and move to the furthest corner of the playground too. It's much quieter in the playground than it was during the morning break. I'm keeping an eye on Harri. If he steps towards me, I move somewhere else. I don't open my mouth; I don't say a word to anyone.

We have singing after dinner. But before that, Mrs Barnwell calls our names and marks the big book again. I listen carefully this time and listen to the children in the next-door class as well, and I'm sure 'He-urr-miss!' is what everyone says in answer to their name. I shudder to think what will happen when my name is read out. The jam sandwich I had for dinner is like a lump of clay in my stomach. I feel my throat hot, closing up, and my tongue receding down to the jam sandwich.

"Roburrt Elees Jowns?"

"He-urr-miss!" That voice again! My mouth is open and ready. I failed to say anything and my mouth is still open as I hear Mrs Barnwell call the name of one of the other boys.

Her eyes are on the far end of our row by now and that's when the dark curly head in front of me turns quickly and looks over her shoulder at me. Only a *chwinciad chwannen* as Dad would say. She looks straight into my eyes – no smile, no frown, nothing. But I know now. Eifiona Jane is my secret voice. Another *chwinciad chwannen*, another 'wink of a flea', and she's turned her head back to face the front. In that half second, I've learned something – more than I've learned in a whole morning of schoolwork. But I can't put it into words, somehow. What's the matter with me? I can't say words and, by now, I can't think in words.

Singing in Ysgol y Llan is not like singing in Sunday school, either. At Sunday school, we open our mouths like horses and sing with gusto and get so much enjoyment from hearing our voices making such a noise together. In Ysgol y Llan we sound as if we're singing about an old dog that's died. I don't know what the song is about, but this is what I hear:

Meh-ri ada lickle lam,
Lickle lam, lickle lam ...

Mrs Barnwell is trying to get the infants who've been in school before to sing the first line, and we who are there for the first time to repeat the words in the second line.

Everyone is mumbling more than singing, with their

heads down so that the words seem to slip through the wooden floorboards under our feet.

"Lickle lam, lickle lam ..."

The only thing I can think of is 'pickles and ham', but I can't sing about them either. There's nothing but a painful grating of breath in my throat as I try to get the sound out.

Mrs Barnwell is moving on and the infants that have been here before sing:

"An evrey-weyr that-meh-ri went
Meh-ri went, meh-ri went ..."

We're supposed to join in with them on the last two words, like before, but somehow all I can hear is the Welsh *mynwent, mynwent* for 'meh-ri went, meh-ri went' and I see Dad in the *mynwent*, with the gravestone lying on top of him and his hand all bloody. I think about the gravestone commemorating all those children buried under it. By the time the singing's over, the room has gone awfully foggy in front of my eyes.

Afternoon playtime consists of more keeping clear and nothing said. A little after everyone is back at their desks for the last lesson, Mr Barnwell gives a shout and points to an empty seat in the third desk from the front of his class. He calls the name Huw Williams, but no one says a thing.

"Huw Williams?" once more, louder this time. The cane comes down and dances on the desk where Huw was sitting earlier in the day.

One of the children says something, and I think he says

that Huw Fron Dirion has gone home.

The headmaster shouts like a madman then and there's a whisper at the back of his class.

Gillian-the-Welsh-Not's hand is in the air like a shot. She says something to the headmaster and stands and points to a stocky boy in the back row. I know him. He's Gareth Tyddyn Dolben. He's in Standard Six and he's a bit older than our Owie. He lives in the farm across the road from us. But Gillian is pointing to him and saying something about *chwynnu maip*.

Gareth Tyddyn Dolben must have said something to the effect that Huw Fron Dirion had gone home to work in the fields as the weather is so nice, and that they hadn't finished weeding turnips – *chwynnu maip* – yet. The headmaster lifts the Welsh Not off Gillian Davies' neck with both hands, like a deacon in chapel walking to the elders' pew with a full collection box. Slowly, he makes Gareth bow his head and the Welsh Not is hung round his neck.

Storytime is the last lesson. No, to be more accurate, the lesson was Mrs Barnwell reading a book to us. Not a story like Miss Elen gives us in Sunday school. No drama, no characters, no excitement. Only the smallest waves of words rise and fall from the book. I almost put my head on the desk and fall asleep, and I'm sure that I would have if Aled hadn't nudged me.

There, the last drama of the day was being performed in front of the whole school.

"Gareth Roberts!" shouted the headmaster, after getting everyone's attention.

Gareth steps forward.

An instruction barked by Mr Barnwell. Gareth holds out his right hand. Whap. Another bark. Gareth holds his left hand out. Whap. Bark. The headmaster hits him with his whole strength on both shoulders and then across the skin of the back of his legs twice.

"Six of the best for speaking Welsh in school!" screams the headmaster.

Gareth hasn't even let out the tiniest of groans to relieve the pain. In an oppressive silence, he gets hold of the Welsh Not and lifts it over his head. He steps towards the big desk and tosses the piece of wood onto it and then walks out of the door. For a second, the headmaster is not sure what to do. Then he seizes the bell to signify that school is over for the day.

I didn't know it at the time, but that was the last time anyone saw Gareth at school. He would be thirteen in November and the kiddie catcher never caught him in Tyddyn Dolben's fields to send him back to school. Ysgol y Llan had hit him for the last time.

Once Aled and I were through the school gate and crossing the footbridge, he started talking non-stop. It was as if someone had uncorked a bottle.

"Do you think we'll get the Welsh Not some day, Bob?"

I looked at him and wondered how on earth I was going to answer him.

"If I get it," I said at last, amazed that my voice had come back. "If I get it, I'll never snitch on you so that it's put round your neck."

"Hey, Bob!" said a girl's voice behind us. "You've got a tongue in your head after all!"

I turn my head to see Gwyneth and Eifiona walking along the path behind us. It was Gwyneth who had spoken. There is no expression on Eifiona's face. I turn back straight away, feeling my cheeks getting hot and my neck sweating.

"Are you going to say something in school tomorrow or is Eifiona-Voice-of-Bob here going to speak for you again?"

My throat has closed up again. But closed up in a different way, somehow. At the main road, Aled and the girls cross together but I wait for Owie to go up the Uwch Afon road together.

At the top of the Uwch Afon bank, as we turn towards the upland where our house lies, we see Dei Coch beside the spring. He's clearing the overgrowth around it, cutting the hedge and resetting the stones where the water collects. He works for the county council as a 'lengthsman', and he's responsible for the drains, walls and hedges along the country roads this side of Llangernyw.

"How are the big lads today?" asks Dei Coch brightly as we approach. "Did you learn anything worthwhile in that old school today? Wouldn't it have been better for you to have had a rake each and given me a hand tidying this hedge, eh?"

"Hello, Dei, how are you?" says Owie. "What are you doing to our well?"

"Clearing around it, see? It'll be easier for you to get to it now."

"But the water's dirty, Dei!" I say.

"Only temporarily, Bob!" Dei's laughing and his mop of

red hair bobs about as he does. "Some of the side stones had fallen in. Let the water settle and it'll be clearer than ever. Whose turn is it to carry water to the house tonight?"

"Bob," says Owie, quick as a flash.

"Owie," I say.

Dei Coch laughs again, before looking more serious and asking "And how's your father now, lads?"

"The same, Dei," answers Owie. "In bed and his back's very bad."

"Give him my regards, lads, give him my best." Dei turns back to his work and positions a large rock in its place on the wall of the well.

Chapter 8

It's Nain Bicycle who meets us at the gate to our house when we get home.

"Boys, how did it go at school today?"

Neither of us gives her a proper answer, we just make a sound like murmuring wasps.

"Did the first day go alright, Bob? Did you make new friends? Owie – what are these streaks on your cheeks, you look like you've been crying?"

Without further ado Nain ushers us into the house and sits us down at the table.

"Pancakes first, and you can tell me all about it afterwards," she says, heading for the griddle on the range where one of Nain's thin pancakes is curling nicely in the heat. Using her pinafore to hold them, she takes hot plates of already-cooked pancakes out of the oven next to the fire.

"There you are, boys. Butter, sugar and lemon on the table. Oh! Go and wash your hands first!"

My hands and Owie's are as black as if we'd been playing with coal all day. It's the slate dust from writing – to clean our slates we have to spit on our fingers and rub the slate with them. Half a minute's scrubbing with soap and water and our hands are clean enough to spread sugar and lemon on the pancakes and gobble them up as if we haven't a moment to spare.

Mmm! Nothing's as good as Nain's pancakes. We don't usually have them unless we have company. This is brilliant – only Owie and me to devour them, without having to share them with anyone or offer visitors the plate first. Very soon, only one pancake is left and Owie and I are both eyeing it while gulping down what we have; the first to finish will claim the prize. Owie wins but as luck would have it Nain empties the last of the batter onto the griddle at that very moment, so I get the warmest pancake!

"Right, what's been happening?" asks Nain, sitting down at the table with us after we've finished feasting. Bit by bit she hears the story of the caning that started Owie's day.

"That old Welsh Not!" spits Nain, and I'm sure she swore under her breath. "I say to you – remember Ceiriog's words:

'Llywelyn *bach* come here
At my knee to learn
Your mother's language first of all
And then Victoria's tongue.'

And what about you, Bob *bach* – did they catch you saying anything in Welsh today?"

"No, Nain," I say. "I never said a single word of Welsh while I was in school."

"Were you too frightened, lovey?"

"Yes, Nain." I didn't mention that I'd not said a word in any language while I was there.

"Look, lads." Nain says, after a moment. "You have to play the fox. You know what I mean?"

"The big boys went to Hafodunnos woods to play the fox during school dinner time last spring," Owie says. "I was too young to go then but I'm sure I can go this year."

"The fox keeps its head when Donald MacDonald the keeper and the hunt are after it," explains Nain. "Maybe he'll head for Coed Rhan Hir as far as Twlc stream, go into the water, walk back down towards the stream Rhan Hir stream, and then turn and go into Coed Hafodunnos and follow the Collen brook up towards Rhos-y-mawn."

"But that's a lot of ground for us to cover in a school dinner time, Nain!" says Owie. "We wouldn't be back until the bell for afternoon playtime!"

"That's the way of the fox, my lad," explains Nain. "Giving the appearance of going one way but heading for somewhere else."

"I don't understand you either, Nain," I say.

"Inside the school, it's the Welsh Not. In the playground, it's the Welsh Not. Am I right so far?" Nain asks.

We both nod our heads.

"If the *sgwlyn* had his way, it'd be the Welsh Not in the village and on the way home too," adds Owie.

"That's where the fox comes into it," Nain explains. "Don't get caught in school or in the playground, you'll get your chance in other places. 'If you can't be strong, be crafty.' Have you heard that saying?"

"Where do you get all these sayings, Nain?" I ask.

"You've got two ears, same as I have, haven't you?" Nain says. "Listen and learn. In the village, in chapel – and in school. Learn things and remember them, and then choose your path carefully."

The taste of the pancakes is still sweet in my mouth as Owie and I quietly reflect on what Nain has said. Then, breaking the silence, we hear the bed in Mam and Dad's bedroom creak and Dad's groan as he tries to move.

"Is Dad any better?" asks Owie.

"You can go and see him. Go on, go through."

"Where's Mam?" I ask.

"She's popped to the Siop Fawr in the village to buy things the doctor said your dad needed," Nain replies quickly and shepherds us through to the bedroom at the back of the house.

Dad is on his side in bed, and it's clear he hasn't been able to get up all day. He attempts a smile when he sees us, but he's biting his lip at the same time.

"How did it go, lads?"

"Very well, Dad," Owie says. "How's the back?"

"It'll be better tomorrow, I'm sure," he answers.

"Did the doctor come to our house?" I can't remember the doctor ever calling here before. Only people with money to pay the doctor have him call at the house. We must have enough money somewhere, it seems.

"Yes, we had to call the doctor, unfortunately," Nain says.

"And what did he say?" Owie asks.

"Plenty of rest," answers Nain.

"I'll be as right as rain in a couple of days," Dad says, trying to cheer us up.

But things weren't better in a couple of days. Not in Dad's bedroom. Not in school either.

Mam had bought some sort of cloths in the Siop Fawr and had received something called a 'poultice', she said, from the doctor. It was something that smelled bad and was spread with a knife onto the cloths, newly boiled in a pot on the fire. Then it was carried, steaming, to be tied round the bottom of Dad's back. The heat of the poultice was supposed to shift the badness that was giving Dad so much pain and preventing him bending his back and using his legs. But now it was Thursday evening and Dad was still in bed.

In school, I quieten down as I cross the footbridge and I fail to say a word until I cross back on my way home. Owie says nothing in the playground either, but I notice he leaves the playground at dinner time and goes to 'play fox' in the streams behind the village until the bell rings. They come back to school a dishevelled gang and looking happy but, but then they sit quietly at their desks for the rest of the afternoon.

Eifiona sits in the row in front of me and Aled sits beside me every day. When Mrs Barnwell calls 'Roburrt Elees Jowns?' the voice in front of me quickly says 'He-urr-miss!' every morning and afternoon. When we have to stand up to say our letters and our numbers, my mouth goes into the right shape but not a peep comes out of me. By now this isn't a problem because Mrs Barnwell doesn't come round us individually and ask for answers, as I've seen Miss Elen and Mr Barnwell do with their classes.

As I cross the footbridge every morning, I look up at the

church and the churchyard. When we were there cutting the grass the previous Saturday, Dad had said to us as we sat under the yew tree for a break:

"You know what, boys? I like coming to this churchyard to work. It's full of Llangernyw people, and I remember a few of them. They kind of keep me company while I'm working here. Then again, they're mute. They never say a word as I tidy round their graves. But then again, after I've been here for a bit, I think I know what they're saying to me too! They're mute people who speak all the time. Do you understand things like that, eh?"

No, I didn't understand what he was getting at on Saturday. But by Thursday, crossing the bridge to school, I was saying to myself – You, too, are one of these mute people now, Bob. I don't think Owie knows anything about this.

On the footbridge, the same thing happens again. The porridge in my stomach turns into a cold stone and sits heavily. Something grips my insides and that knot, in its turn, climbs inside me until it reaches my throat. My throat constricts, closing my windpipe. If Nain were to offer me sweet pancakes at that moment, I wouldn't be able to eat them. And I certainly wouldn't be able to thank her for them. Then the inside of my throat stays tight all day. I have no voice at all. I make sure I've been to the toilet before I reach school and during playtime and dinner time because I have no voice – let alone no English – to ask to be excused during the lessons.

Am I sick? I don't know. Maybe I should have a cloth and poultice round my throat, like Dad has on his back. But afterwards, on crossing the footbridge on the way home, the knot, the tightness and the stone all disappear. It's not a cloth and a poultice I need, then. But what?

Before tea, Owie and I go to see Dad. He wants to know which English words I've learned at school that day.

"I learned 'wun, tŵ, thri' today, Dad," I'll say. Or, "I learned 'dog' for *ci* and 'cat' for *cath* today, Dad."

"Good lad," and he'll smile from his bed, stuck on his back.

I can remember and say the English words fine in Dad's bedroom but I can't say them in school. I'm not refusing to say them. I want to say them like everyone else. Aled glances at me sometimes when we're on our feet and saying the words together, but he never mentions it on the way home. Eifiona and Gwyneth walk in front of us up the path to the main road, and sometimes they walk behind us. On the Thursday afternoon, Gwyneth turns back towards us and she is on the point of saying something – something about Eifiona-Voice-of-Bob, probably – when Eifiona gives her a punch in the arm. She shuts her mouth then.

What's wrong with me? I cannot talk, rather than refuse to talk. Maybe first-week nerves is all it is, and I'll be fine next week. I'm pleased it's Thursday afternoon. Very pleased. No school tomorrow – it's the day of the grouse shoot on Mynydd Moelogan.

When we reach the main road, Eifiona turns to Owie and me and asks:

"Is where you live good for playing hide-and-seek?"

"Coed Twlc is a brilliant place," says Owie. "Lots of hollows and big tree trunks."

"Can we come over after tea?" asks Eifiona. "Will you come with me, Gwyneth?"

"Can I come too?" asks Aled.

"But Owie, we have to ..." I'm about to remind Owie of all the things we have to do because Dad's bed-bound.

"What's wrong with you now, then?" asks Eifiona, and I feel like I always have some big problem.

*　*　*

After tea, the three of them arrive at Bronrhwylfa. Owie and I are waiting for them in the road.

"Come on! This way!" shouts Owie, running to meet them and turning to the left.

The path takes us past Tyddyn Twlc, a small farm where two old brothers, John and Owen Elis, live.

"What a name for a house: 'Twlc' – doesn't it mean 'pigsty'?" says Gwyneth as we pass.

Down by the stream is a large tree.

"This will do as a counting tree," says Owie. "You go and hide – this side or the other side of the stream – but you must be able to see this tree before hiding, alright?"

Owie starts to count to twenty. We scurry off in all directions.

"Twenty ... Coming, ready or not!" Owie shouts.

I'm crouching behind a big tree trunk fairly close to the stream, but on the other side. I know that Owie will be scanning in all directions first. He soon shouts:

"Gwyneth! I can see your blue dress to the right of that tree over there! Seen you, Gwyneth!"

"No you can't, I'm hidden," Gwyneth answers. There's a noisy argument for a while but then she gives in.

I can hear Owie prowling about near the stream. He's clever enough to search in a circle close by him and then slowly work his way outwards. He's upstream now and getting further away every second, and I'm about to give him a chance when I hear the sound of rushing.

"Aled! I've seen you!" Owie shouts.

"First to the counting tree!" shouts Aled.

I venture a peep over the bracken that's around my tree trunk and I see Aled and Owie racing from two different directions and both are yelling like mad. Owie wins. He has longer legs.

I pop my head back down once I see Owie following the stream down this time. He's walking quietly and it's difficult to place him. I'm dying to raise my head again but then I hear a scream as Eifiona jumps when he finds her hiding place. Then there's another noisy race and I take advantage of that to leave my tree trunk and run to one that's closer to the stream. I'm in a good position to reach the counting tree next time. Aled can see me, but I put my finger to my lips.

Just then, there's a shout much louder and much deeper than our playful shouts.

"Get out of my woods!"

That's Mac's voice, I think to myself. I ease up enough to be able to squint through the bracken with one eye. The red-headed gamekeeper is charging along the path from the direction of the Plas with his gun lying across his arm. The mark on his face is a fierce purple. He's ranting and raging, but before he's close enough to catch my friends or see their faces properly, the four have made a run for Tyddyn Twlc as fast as their legs will carry them.

I can hear the gamekeeper slowing down beside the stream. He's grousing and swearing under his breath but he doesn't give chase any further. At long last, he turns and goes back in the direction of Coed y Plas. I wait for ages and I'm about to get up when I hear the sound of feet coming along the path again.

I hide once more. These are cautious feet. They're not rushing wildly like Mac's. They pass and go on towards Coed y Plas. By and by I lift my head and look. I recognise Ifan my brother's back! What is he doing, alone, in Coed y Plas? But I don't dare shout after him in case I attract the attention of the gamekeeper again.

Chapter 9

The next morning I hear Mam's voice in the kitchen; she's talking to Dad.

"What on earth are you doing up, Wil?"

"It's the grouse shoot today, isn't it, Lisa? The Colonel and the keepers need me with them today."

"But your back, Wil!"

"Never mind that, it'll be light duties today, won't it," I hear my father reply. "No scything, no carrying stones, no opening drains with a pickaxe. Just a little walk on the mountain with the lah-di-dahs in their deerstalkers – not that we have deer – and their plus fours like bloomers. That's all."

I think Mam is about to snap back at him, when I open the door of our bedroom and walk into the kitchen.

"You're better, Dad!"

Mum sees the joyful smile on my face and turns away.

"Better enough for what I'll be called on to do today, Bob," says Dad. "Yes indeed, good enough for the Glorious Twelfth."

"What exactly is it all about, Dad?"

"It's the twelfth of August today," explains Dad, as he winds a sack tightly round his bare midriff and secures it at the front with safety pins. "This is the first day it's legal to go onto the mountain to shoot grouse. The law lets them nest in peace and raise their chicks until they can fly properly before the shooting season starts, you see."

"Why do we need lah-di-dahs to shoot them? Why can't the farmers and the keepers shoot them?" I ask.

"Oh, you need expensive guns to be able to hit them, don't you, Dad?" Owie has got up and has now joined us in the kitchen.

"I don't know about that, but you need a very good aim. They fly low and fast, you see."

"Faster than a racing horse, don't they, Dad?" Owie says.

"A lot faster, and they can turn this way and that on the wing. It's quite a contest, and the lah-di-dahs come here from far and wide and pay the Colonel at the Plas dearly so they can show off with their guns."

"The Colonel'll make a fortune today, won't he, Dad? says Owie.

"It's an important day for him, that's for sure," Dad says. "But remember they've been working towards this all winter. Do you remember me going up onto the moors to burn the old heather in February? Well that's part of the work of making sure the grouse get young heather shoots to eat. And then every keeper on the estate catches foxes and weasels and kills magpies and birds of prey, so that the grouse chicks get a chance. They nest on the ground, under the branches of the heather, so foxes can just help themselves. It all costs the estate."

"Weather doesn't look too good for the lah-di-dahs today, Dad," says Owie, who's opened the door at Bronrhywlfa and is looking across at Moel Derwydd, Moel Gydia and Mynydd Moelogan. After a week of scorching hot weather, there are black clouds over the mountains.

"Looks like it'll be unsettled," Dad says. "A storm's brewing after this hot spell we've had. The sooner the guns are on the mountain, the better."

Dad is trying to put on his flannel shirt over the sack, but he's having trouble with the sleeves and Mam has to slowly guide his arms to the right place.

"Are you sure you're able to do what's needed today, Wil?" Mam's asking him.

"Only walk and keep an eye on things, that's all I do," Dad answers. "Very light work. This sack'll keep my back straight as I walk."

"Who's got to run with the first grouse for them to catch the train?" asks Mam.

"One of the young lads can do that."

"Why do the grouse want to catch the train, Dad?" I ask.

"Today is the first chance for posh restaurants in London to serve grouse to their rich customers, you see. The Colonel usually has an order for about four dozen, to go straight to London from Llanrwst on the train, so they'll be on the plates of lords by tonight. Costs a fortune, as you can imagine. But then they can brag that they've had roast grouse on the Glorious Twelfth."

"What did they do before there was a train from Llanrwst, Dad?" I'm trying to imagine horses racing towards London with sacks of grouse.

"It's something that started with the age of rail. Back in your *taid*'s days, to tell you the truth. Right, where's my jacket? Have you got your sticks ready, lads? The Plas wagon will be here in no time."

The previous evening, Owie and I had cut two stout sticks, the length of our legs, in the wood behind the house. We went into the road to wait for the wagon and before long we could hear its wheels crunching the gravel as it climbed towards Bronrhwylfa. It's Tommy the Carrier driving and he's rather surprised to see Dad there as well. Tommy's got a good strong horse to pull the wagon, in which there are already about six lads and their sticks. Aled is one of them and I'm glad I'll be in his company on a very different day to a school day.

We're a very jolly company in the wagon as we go onwards along the brow of the hill. Dad's up front with Tommy the Carrier, who's asking earnestly about his back. We in the back are singing 'Bonheddwr Mawr o'r Bala'. Like me, this is the first time that Aled has joined the beaters, and we're determined to enjoy ourselves.

After about a mile, we stop at the door of a farm called Wenlli and two more lads climb into the wagon. The older one is Gwilym Wenlli and it looks to me as if he is leading the beaters today. He starts telling us what to do.

"We'll be standing in a long row, about ten steps between us on the top of the mountain. I'll be at the upper end and I'll be waiting for a sign from Mac that the guns are in place. That's what they call the people shooting: 'the guns'. I give you a sign then and the beating starts. We move together – it's important that no one lags behind or the grouse will escape in the wrong direction, through the gap. We'll be shaking the bushes, stamping the earth with our feet and shouting until the birds rise in the direction of the guns. And you stop when I say so – or you may be the joint on a London platter tonight!

"What do you think it'll do, Wil?" Tommy's discussing the weather with Dad. "Will it hold?"

By now we're looking down into the gap of the Conwy Valley below us, heading for Tyrpeg Uchaf. There's low cloud in the valley and the sky is black above the hills.

"There'll be a storm, guaranteed," says Dad. "These beaters had better be flush the birds pretty quick, I'd say."

*   *   *

We are standing in a line in the heather, which comes up to my waist. From the shoulder of the mountain down to a torrent in a dip, the pattern is a big lad and a little lad every other. Gwilym Wenlli is closest to the brow of the hill. Over in the valley from us the clouds are churning, like some giant with stomach ache.

Hidden from our view, we know that there are about fifteen of the lah-di-dahs in their shooting gear. Dad and Tommy have helped them strap on their cartridge belts and load them beside the two coaches that had brought them up from the Plas and from the Stag inn in Llangernyw, where they had stayed last night. Word was that there would be a big after-shoot supper party in the Plas tonight.

I see Mac coming across towards Gwilym Wenlli. He has a gun over his arm and his eyes are fiery. The red, purple and yellow marks on the dry skin on his left cheek look angry, making him look more threatening than usual. Without pausing, he fires a few questions at Gwilym. I would think he's checking that everyone knows what their job is. His eyes are still wild and his ginger eyebrows frown. He has a belt of cartridges across his chest and as he walks away I see him draw two of them out and load his gun.

My last glimpse of Dad is seeing him and Tommy carrying a big basket of food between them, and two keepers doing the same thing with another basket, towards the shooting box at the summit of Mynydd Moelogan. Owie comments that the people on the shoot get enough food and drink on a day like this. Dad is holding the basket with one hand and trying to keep his back straight with the other but he's hobbling badly, even so.

A call comes from the hill above our heads – Gwilym signals for us to start walking and beating. The birds rise up from the earth straight away – there must be hundreds on these slopes. They call and scream as they fly up, something that sounds like 'go-bac, go-bac, go-bac!' I'm walking, banging the ground and waving my stick – it's hard work for someone my size, with tough heather branches threatening to drown me sometimes. But I manage to keep the line straight and the air is full of rising, swirling birds.

There are the first shots. We are gradually climbing as we beat, and before long we can see the line of guns, each holding their weapon straight out from the shoulder. Firing two shots. Weapon down, reload with cartridges. Aim and fire again. The sound is deafening. The birds fly low and fast but plenty of them fall.

There's a white flag being raised.

"Stop!" shouts Gwilym. The firing continues until the last

bird has gone past and the white flag is raised again. I see Dad and Tommy letting the black dogs loose. They will run out to pick up the birds and carry them back to be put in the sacks. Before long I see Tommy hoist a sack onto his back and walk towards one of the Plas coaches. That's the sack that'll be on its way to London by train, I should think.

Then Mac is shouting something and waving one arm madly. He's pointing the gun into the air with the other hand.

"Come on," says Gwilym. "They're in a hurry to get more shooting done before the weather turns. Hurry up. Down the stream and work our way up in the same direction."

We beat four parts of the hill before dinner.

"Keep it up, laddies. No time to waste," says Mac, as he passes us while we're eating our sandwiches – although I don't understand a word. White bread sandwiches too – we're eating like lah-di-dahs!

After two more lines of beating after dinner, it has got so dark that it is difficult to see the guns at the top of the hill. Then, like a gunshot, a yellow streak of lightning cracks above our heads. Five seconds later, a huge smack of thunder behind us. One of the keepers raises the white flag on the hillside and waves it frantically.

"They're stopping!" shouts Gwilym. "They want us to go back up. It must be too dangerous on the open hill here because of the lightning."

There's another flash of lightning, forked like an antler. Here on the hilltops we can see for miles. That lightning slashed through the gloom and we'd seen see a flash of light on Moel Derwydd.

"That one hit the ground," says Owie as he pants up the hill next to me. "It wasn't far away, either."

"Chuck your sticks away!" shouts Gwilym. "We'll be faster then."

Four seconds, then thunder.

"Count the seconds," says Owie. "For every second between the lightning and the thunderclap, the storm is a mile away from us."

By the time we reach the brow of the hill, red-cheeked and out of breath, we see that the lah-di-das are all in the shooting box and Dad and Tommy are by the door holding the guns. The last of the deerstalker caps is disappearing inside and he places his gun on top of the pile that is already in Dad's outstretched arms.

"Why are they leaving their guns, Owie?" I ask.

"Metal attracts lightning, doesn't it? The lah-di-dahs are safer in the shooting box without their steel guns," Owie replies.

"Will that lightning come through the air and hit the guns Dad and Tommy have?"

"It could," says Owie. "We're high on the hill. The lightning's looking for a place to hit the earth and the gun is a conductor."

"But what about Dad and Tommy?"

At that, lightning illuminates the sky behind the shooting box.

"Come on! Use your head!"

As we are running for the shooting box, Mac appears, hurtling in the same direction. He's at the door before us. We see one of the party coming through the doorway and take hold of Mac's gun, intending to add it to Dad's pile, I would think.

"Let go o' ma gun!" roars Mac, whipping back and aiming the barrel of his gun to threaten the owner of the hand. The owner of the hand hastily retreats into the darkness within.

"Nobody takes the gun off me!" growls Mac.

Chapter 10

Mac's still carrying his own gun, and I notice that so are the other gamekeepers.

"Go and get the baskets and skedaddle for to wagon," Mac says to Gwilym and two others. I don't understand a word except 'Go' but I see the lads fetch the food baskets and run towards the track. Some of the other lads are carrying sacks full of grouse. By now Dad and Tommy have started across the hilltop, carrying the guns.

Another shout from Mac and the lah-di-dahs come out of the shooting box and lumber like cattle towards the wagon and the coaches. I see them keeping clear of Dad, Tommy and the weapons.

Lightning and another crack of thunder. Two seconds between them.

Dad's having trouble. He's slowed down and his posture is crooked. Owie's noticed as well.

"Come on, we'll go and help him, Bob."

When we reach Dad, Owie takes three of the guns and puts them across my arms. Then he gets hold of five more himself.

"Come along, hurry."

Dad is hobbling the best he can through the heather. I try to make headway but I can't see anything in front of me except the shiny gun barrels. Owie's voice is a little ahead of us now and he's shouting at us to get a move on.

Lightning, and thunder right on its tail. I suddenly feel a huge drop of rain hit my cheek. Another on my arm.

"Gimme here, laddie. What a bunch of cowards are these lairds and colonels, eh? Sassenachs!"

I hadn't heard his approach, but it's Mac beside me, gesturing at the light Plas carriages with their cargo of lah-di-dahs already departing swiftly down the track. He takes the guns from me, turns to look at Dad and says, "Go and help your father."

Then he goes to relieve Owie of some of his load.

I understand 'help' too and so I offer my shoulder to Dad, put my arm round his waist and try to get him to the wagon as quickly as possible.

By the time we arrive, the rain is hammering down. The raindrops are bouncing wildly on the track and the wagon. The gamekeepers and all the gear are arrayed around the wagon.

Mac is shouting commands like a madman. We pack the sacks of birds and the under the driver's seat, then the food baskets inside. The other gamekeepers sit on those and then we boys are crammed in round each other and the dogs on the floor. Mac, Dad and Tommy are on the driver's seat and at last we start for Tyrpeg Uchaf.

The horses can't trot with such a weight on board and we lads have to walk up the Wenlli hill to lessen the load. Well before we reach home, every one of us is soaked to the skin. Anyone would think we'd been hunting fish, not grouse.

In front of Bronrhwylfa the wagon stops for us to get

down. I notice Mac ease his shoulder under Dad's arm to help him down from the driver's seat and support him through the rain to the door of the house. Mam has opened it, ready for us. The rain is still teeming down. As Mac leaves, he gives Owie and me a shilling each and says something that sounds like "Thanks, laddies," before running back through the storm to the wagon.

In front of the fire, Mam is helping Dad out of his jacket and shirt and opening the pins that are holding the sack round his middle. He dries himself on a towel and in no time he's into his flannel nightshirt and in bed. When I go into the bedroom with a mug of hot tea and some bread for him, there are pearls of sweat on his forehead and his smile is very weak.

"You've got a fever, Wil," says Mam. "You're to stay in that bed for a few days."

We weren't to know it at the time, but Dad hardly moved from his bed for the next three years. The pain in his back worsened and he found it difficult to hold a spoon, let alone a spade. A farm labourer who can't lift a sheep or make a hole in the ground with a crowbar is of no use to anyone. Mam had to go on parish relief, receiving five shillings' dole a week to keep the house and family and make ends meet.

*   *   *

All that was still ahead of us. Later that afternoon, Jac was the next to arrive, looking rather like and drowned rat. Nain Bicycle must have been on the look out for him because he'd only just taken his sopping clothes off when she bowled in to see what sort of week it had been for him in town.

"I've got a new name, for starters," Jac says.

"What's that, Jac?" Nain asks.

Jac holds up his winter trousers that Mam stitched for him the previous weekend.

"I'm Jac Two-Trousers now!"

"Oh! They're a bunch of scoundrels!" Nain says.

"It doesn't matter," Jac says. "No one else in the school has anything like these. I'm sure they're jealous, really."

"Don't worry, we'll try and get you some new trousers before the end of the year," Mam says.

We didn't know it at the time, but my brother was to remain Jac Two-Trousers for the rest of his time at big school. Within the year, he'd had to stop lodging in town and had to borrow Nain's bicycle to travel to and from school in all weathers.

Jac wants to know every detail about the first few days at school. Everything went quiet as I told them that the worst thing so far had been seeing Owie being caned for trying to show me the ropes on the first day.

"They have an extremely strange way of thinking," says Jac, after a pause. "They think there's only enough room in our heads for one language and a few other words of a dead language like Latin. They think that by beating Welsh out of us they're making room for English."

"That's exactly what I read," says Nain Bicycle. "'That speaking Welsh in day schools, in the most rural areas of Wales years ago was a dire offence.' That was what it said in the magazine. But it's still is an offence in Ysgol y Llan, isn't it? Why, Jac?"

"The Welsh Not – 'you must not speak Welsh'," Jac says in English, continuing in Welsh, "which some schools in Wales have now stopped using. There's a very discerning man who's doing a lot for the children of Wales by trying his best to get teachers and headteachers here to teach the history of Wales and our own poetry in our schools. Owen Edwards is his name."

"I've heard of him!" Nain says. "He's the one who's behind the *Cymru Coch* magazine, and the one for children, *Cymru'r Plant*, isn't he? I buy them in Llanrwst fair every month, and I've kept every copy of *Cymru'r Plant* since it started, twelve years ago. They were worth their weight in gold for keeping Bob here entertained when he was ill in bed."

"Is that where you get your stories from, Nain?" Owie asks.

"Yes, most of them," chuckles Nain. "And my silly imagination!" She turns to me and asks, "What went to London on its head?"

There was a great silence in the house, then I see Jac rocking and hiding his laughter behind his hand. I had the feeling he'd read *Cymru'r Plant* in Nain's house.

"I don't know, Nain."

"A nail in a horseshoe!" Nain Bicycle has a particularly silly laugh when she says things like this.

"Good, eh? I'm telling you, every edition of *Cymru'r Plant* is as good as a month of education in school."

"Better, if anything," Jac says. "Welsh songs, the history of European countries in Welsh, stuff about the stars and natural history – it's all in there."

"It was in one copy that I got that information about the bat," Nain says. "You two'll have to start coming over and having a leaf through them, like Jac did years ago."

"Did you learn to read Welsh in school, Nain?" I ask.

"Goodness me, no. There was no opportunity to go to school. There was no law to make everyone get an education in those days. The place for girls like me was to be home to help in the house and around our smallholding. Only a few boys went to school, where there was a bit of money in the family."

"So how did you get to read so well and to be so keen on reading to us, Nain?" Owie asks.

"Cledwyn Saer's mother taught me in her Sunday school class," Nain replies, with a faraway look in her eyes. "The best gift I ever had in my life. I've had hours and hours of pure pleasure. And even more pleasure later, reading to my children and grandchildren. And when *Cymru'r Plant* started, well, I was in seventh heaven!"

"But why don't Mr Barnwell and everyone else in school use those, then?" Owie asks.

"There are some – no, that's not true – there are many, here in Wales, who think that teaching anything through Welsh is a waste of time," Jac says. "Welsh is fine for talking to the pigs and the calves in, and for shouting at the dog – but you must acquire English to do everything else. You must have English to get on in the world."

"That's what Guto Bontsyllty told me outside chapel once," Owie says. "Welsh is fine for going to Llanrwst fair, but if you want to go to Abergele fair or further, you must have English."

"What Owen Edwards says is that it's important to have both languages," says Jac. "He's travelled through Europe and speaking two languages is very commonplace there. He says that having two languages is like having two windows in a wall. We see twice as much, and twice as far, through two windows, and twice as much light comes into the room. People who speak only English are those with only one window, and unfortunately many, many of our teachers think that one window's sufficient."

"What's 'Sassenachs', Jac?" I suddenly ask.

"Where did you hear that, Bob?"

"On the hill this afternoon," I reply. "That's what Mac the keeper called the lah-di-dahs that were shooting grouse when they passed all their guns to Dad and Tommy."

"'Sassenachs' is what people from Scotland call the English," explains Jac. "Usually it's not used to be friendly."

"It's an English word, then?"

"No, the Scots have their own language like we Welsh. 'Sassenachs' is a Gaelic word. Mac comes from the Isle of Skye right in the north of Scotland, and Gaelic was his everyday language when he was a little boy."

"He has his own language like us, then?" I say, amazed.

"Yes. And he says something in it every now and again. Proverbs usually, to try and explain something. And then he translates them into English for our benefit."

"Oh! Proverbs!" Nain Bicycle loves things like that. "Come on, give us an example then!"

"If you burn your backside in front of the fire, it's only you who has to sit on it!" recites Jac.

"I like it!" Nain says. "Worth remembering after today's soaking in the storm."

"The people are stronger than the king – that's another one of his."

"That's like a Welsh one – 'The land is stronger than the lord' – isn't it?"

"Two languages that share the same roots, you see," Jac says. "But as it is here, lots of teachers in schools in Scotland ban Gaelic and if you speak it in school you get the cane."

"Did Mac get the cane for speaking Gaelic like Owie got it for speaking Welsh?" I ask.

"I wouldn't be surprised," Jac says.

This is what we talked about late into that evening. A little before dusk, the storm had cleared and the sunset was spectacular. The midges weren't biting either – a good sign that the rain had cleared, according to Nain Bicycle.

After shutting the hens up and feeding the pigs, I notice that two grouse have been left on our garden gatepost and I take them inside, to a very surprised Mam.

Chapter 11

I thought that some things looked fairly bright by the end of that first week in Ysgol y Llan. Having heard about Owie's punishment, Jac asked me if I had been caught speaking Welsh in school yet and had received a warning.

"No, Jac, I haven't been caught. To tell you the truth, I haven't said a word of Welsh since I've been there, either," I was able to say honestly.

"That's a very difficult thing, Bob. If you can bite your tongue, so much the better," answered Jac, "it's what I have to do all the time in the County School in Llanrwst."

Jac doesn't know that there's no need for me to bite my tongue. The sound of the words don't reach my tongue. They are stuck deep inside me.

But my predicament is brought home to me on Sunday morning, on seeing that Eifiona is not at Sunday school. She's poorly, her mother tells Elen Jones; she's caught cold after being out in the storm. Will she be in school tomorrow to answer for me?

* * *

Before the bell rings the next day, I scan the playground but it's clear that Eifiona isn't there.

Bell. Line up and in we go. There isn't a space in front of

me, as Gwyneth is sitting in Eifiona's place, but I see a huge gap anyway.

As Mrs Barnwell calls the girls' names, there's a silence after she says 'Eifiona Jane Edwards'. That silence pains me.

The boys come next. What will I do? There's a stone in my stomach, a rope round my guts and the cave that is my throat has closed up tightly, just as before.

"Roburrt Elees Jowns?"

I'm unable to say anything. There's no one to answer on my behalf, either. The only thing I can do is raise my hand. Mrs Barnwell sees it and I nod my head.

"Yes, boy?"

I'm unable to reply. I look down, still nodding my head.

I sense her getting up from her desk and coming to stand in front of the rows of desks.

"Yes, boy," she says again, this time her voice is closer and less patient.

Fair play to Aled, he tries to save me by pointing at me and saying: "Robat Elis Jôs, miss."

"Let him answer for himself."

Aled points at my throat and says "Noh ..."

"He hasn't got any voice?"

"Noh, miss."

I shake my head.

"Are you ill?"

I have no idea what she's asked me, but I keep on shaking my head from side to side.

"But you don't have a voice?"

I'm still shaking my head.

By now, most of the other class nearest to us – Elen Jones' class – has turned to look at the drama being played out. Mrs Barnwell turns to its teacher.

"Miss Elen, is this boy in your chapel class?"

"Yes, Mrs Barnwell."

"Do you know if he has a voice or not?"

"He seemed alright yesterday, Mrs Barnwell."

I have no idea what's being said, but I see Elen Jones' discomfort and that she is now looking at the floor. Mrs Barnwell turns back to me.

"Did you have a voice to speak in chapel yesterday, boy?" She shoots this question at me, but because by now I have no idea what's happening, I neither nod nor shake my head.

"Answer me, boy!"

I can't move a muscle by now.

"Miss Elen tells me you had a voice yesterday." She raises her voice to look at the whole class. "Has any of you heard Robert Elis Jones' voice in school today?"

No one puts up their hand. She turns back to me and signals for me to stand up.

"Stand up and say 'Here, miss'."

I look at her lips moving. She repeats the words, but louder this time: "Say 'Here, miss'!"

I understand what she's trying to get me to do. The 'He-urr-miss' is there inside me, but I can't get it out through my throat. I can make the shapes with my mouth and that's what I do now. She cranes her neck towards me.

"Louder boy, I can't hear you!"

I mouth 'He-urr-miss' again, but without a sound coming out of my lips.

"LOUDER, BOY!"

After I've made the right shapes with my mouth for a third time, I notice the headmaster himself walking over to us.

"Any trouble, Mrs Barnwell?"

"This boy won't say 'Here, miss' when I call the register."

"Won't or can't? Are you refusing to answer, boy?" I understand he's asking me something, because he's calling me 'boy', but I can't nod or shake my head.

"He might have lost his voice since yesterday," suggests Mrs Barnwell.

"We'll give him the benefit of the doubt for today," says Mr Barnwell, "and see how he is tomorrow. Sit down, boy."

As he's gesturing for me to sit, I sit down. Mrs Barnwell goes back to her desk and finishes reading the register. The lessons follow their usual pattern and I make the usual shapes with my mouth when necessary. When the register is called after dinner, I put my hand up when I hear my name. Mrs Barnwell raises her head to look at me and then turns back to the rest of the names.

* * *

That afternoon after school, Owie is waiting for Aled and me on the other side of the footbridge.

"How's your voice now, Bob?"

I cough twice and spit into the river.

"A-hem. It's back now, Owie, it's alright."

"What was wrong with you in class, then?"

Aled is at my side straight away.

"There's something wrong with Bob's voice since he started school, Owie. He can't say anything in class or in the playground."

"Is that true, Bob?"

"Yes, Owie. The words don't come out of my mouth. I try my best, but they're not there. I can't sing, either."

"Come on, let's head home and see what Mam and Dad have to say about it."

As we turn to go up the path that leads to the road, I see that Gwyneth, Harri and another couple of children are crossing the bridge.

*　　*　　*

Dad has been in bed all day, and he's doesn't get up to have tea with us either. Over a jam sandwich and buttermilk, Owie tells Mam about the problem.

"Come through and have a word with your dad," Mam says, after she's been at his bedside telling him what's been going on.

"You've got no voice, my boy?" Dad asks.

"Not while I'm at school."

"Is the problem not being able to speak English, or is it that old illness you had when you were little coming back?" he asks.

"Well, I can't speak English, can I, but I try my best. It's just that nothing comes out."

"Could you try a bit more?" asks Mam.

"I try my very best every day."

"Try to swallow your saliva, take a breath and then say the word," Dad suggests. "Will you try that tomorrow?"

"I will, Dad, but I'm not sure it'll work."

"I know it's hard," Mam says, "but every one of the other children has had to go through the same thing, you know. You're not the only one."

*   *   *

"I'm not the only one." These words run through my head the following morning as I hear the names of the girls being called by Mrs Barnwell. Each one of them opens her mouth and gives the expected response with no fuss. Each one except Eifiona. She is absent again today.

I put my hand up when I hear 'Roburrt Elees Jowns'.

Mrs Barnwell looks at me.

I mouth the 'He-urr-miss'.

She gets up from her seat and comes to stand in front of the rows of desks in our part of the classroom.

"Have you lost your voice again today, Robert?"

I nod my head as I stand up.

"No voice since chapel on Sunday eh, boy?"

I work out that she's asking me something about being in chapel on Sunday and so continue nodding.

"Miss!"

The class – and Mrs Barnwell – turn to look at Harri, who has his hand in the air.

"Miss! Robat ... speekio ... Owie ..." and he points to the door and to outside.

"Are you telling me you heard Robert talking to his

brother outside yesterday, Henry?"

"I-ess-miss."

Mrs Barnwell crosses the classroom to have a word with her husband. Mr Barnwell gets up, straightens himself and reaches for one of the canes on his desk. He goes to the blackboard and unhooks the Welsh Not from its peg. He walks across the room as if he's carrying the sacrament in chapel.

"We do not tolerate insolence, boy! Are you being rude to Mrs Barnwell?"

I look at him and my bottom lip starts to quiver.

"Let me hear you say 'Here, miss' loud and clear then," the headmaster commands.

With trembling lips I mouth the words, while looking at the cane and the Welsh Not.

"LOUDER, BOY!"

I can only mouth the right shapes again.

Mr Barnwell looks around the infants' class.

"Which one of you says that he heard this boy talking perfectly naturally yesterday?"

Slowly, Harri raises his hand in the air. Mr Barnwell turns furiously and points at me with the cane.

"Which means that you are refusing to speak English, boy! That is the same as speaking Welsh in school. You will wear this Welsh Not around your neck and follow the usual rules."

He comes to the end of the row. I shuffle up and stick my neck out towards him. I feel the cord digging into the skin of my nape with the weight of the Welsh Not.

Chapter 12

The weight of the Welsh Not on my chest makes me think of the bodies in the churchyard with the weight of the gravestones on their bones. Is this how they feel, I wonder. Imprisoned. Oppressed. 'The silent people'. As well as a stone in my stomach I've got a weight on my heart now.

I stand up with the others to name the letters and the numbers but it's harder to mouth them today. It's impossible to open my throat.

The playtime bell isn't a release today. There's a difference between being left alone and being shunned. I see Owie in the playground from afar and he gives me a thumbs up, but he's can't cross the invisible line between the big boys' area and the infants' area – and me. When I walk towards the wall, to lean on it, those in my class move further away, out of earshot.

It's the same at dinner time, just with fewer in the playground because the big lads are playing fox in the woods. I think about the fox and what Nain said he wanted us to be: 'like the fox'. What would she say to me today, I wonder?

A little before the bell rings to call us back for the afternoon's lessons, Harri runs up to me and points towards one of the girls and says: "Speekio Welsh, Robat – speekio Welsh!"

I look Harri in the eye and I'm not sure what I see there.

Is he trying to save me from the cane? Or is he busily trying to accumulate credit, thinking that only by making accusations against others will he save his own skin? I say nothing and the bell rings.

As we're lined up, the story Jac told us about that education man comes back to me. What was his name again? That was it: Owen M. Edwards from Llanuwchllyn. He had spoken Welsh in school, Jac said, and the teacher had put the Welsh Not round his neck. But Owen Edwards had refused to pass the Welsh Not on to other children he heard speaking Welsh. He had refused to accuse. He had refused to be the school sneak, carrying tales to the teacher.

That meant that Owen Edwards had borne the Welsh Not every day and had been caned every day. In the end, he had given up going to school and had spent his days roaming the countryside and learning about nature. That's how he could write so much about birds, flowers and animals in that *Cymru'r Plant* that Nain Bicycle reads. But he is about the same age as my father, and things were different back then. There were no kiddie catchers to force children to school in those days. Dad didn't go to school much either – it was only through the Sunday school that he managed to learn to read, write and sing songs.

Walking into the classroom, I think about Gareth Tyddyn Dolben tossing the Welsh Not onto the headmaster's desk and making off through the door with no intention of ever coming back to school. But Gareth was almost thirteen years old. I'm not yet eight. And anyway, I could never take the caning without crying, as Gareth had done.

Through the singing lesson, I think how a fox would think, and what Jac would say. I think about the cane as well and I know it's not far off now. But at the same time, I know I can't say a word in school because I'm unable to talk, not that I refuse to talk.

By afternoon playtime, I long to shut myself in the toilet and have a proper cry until it's time to go home. But I don't go there. I'm in a corner of the playground on my own until that Harri comes running towards me again.

"Gwyneth speekio Welsh! Gwyneth speekio Welsh!"

Behind him I see Gwyneth standing on her own in the middle of the yard and she's already starting to cry. Through the lining up and walking inside, she's still crying. A little after we sit down, the girl closest to Gwyneth puts up her hand and draws Mrs Barnwell's attention to something.

"Gwyneth, miss – pee-pee, miss!"

Gwyneth has had an accident.

Mrs Barnwell gives her a mouthful and she has to go back out. When she comes back in, she has to dry the seat and sit there and have a row delivered by Mrs Barnwell again. For the rest of the afternoon, I hear her having another outbreak of sobbing every so often, and getting another telling-off.

With not long to go before the last bell, Mr Barnwell demands the whole school's attention and walks over to our class with his cane. He bows it like a bridge in front of me and starts to preach.

I don't follow what he has to say to us, but the words 'No ... Welsh ... sgool ...' are repeated over and over.

He has a long piece of doggerel, and although I couldn't

understand it at the time, I've heard it often enough since for it to stay with me like a verse from the Bible:

I speak in Welsh to count the sheep,
I shout in Welsh to drive the dogs,
But English is the way to keep
Me clean from mud and mountain bogs;
I'll speak in English in this land
Or strike the cane across my hand.

Next he points at a sign on the wall. With time I learn to read this as well:

No throwing stones in the yard.
No dirty hands in the classroom.
No speaking in Welsh.

By now the headmaster is looking at me in the same way a sheepdog eyes sheep. He motions for me to rise and with the tip of the cane he half lifts the Welsh Not's cord from round my neck. He's asking me something about 'sbeek in Welsh' and I know he's expecting me to point at someone else in class. I look at Harri and I'm sorely tempted to point my finger at him. But I know Harri would hotly dispute the accusation and name Gwyneth, and things would be worse for me in the end. I shake my head.

"Answer properly, boy!" the headmaster yells.

Although I don't understand the words, I know what he's said, so I shake my head and mouth 'Noh-sir'.

"I can't hear you, boy!"

I bow my head.

Then something unexpected happens. I hear Elen Jones' voice saying something quietly to Mr Barnwell. I may not have a voice, but my ears hear well enough. She's saying something about 'furst tie-m'.

And the headmaster uses the cane to remove the Welsh Not from round my neck by its cord. In doing so he makes sure that I feel the grain of the cane on my cheek so I get the sense of the stick on my skin. I hear 'furst tie-m' and 'warning' and 'last tie-m' and he nods towards the boy who rings the bell.

I go out of the door and across the yard like a bullet to catch up with Owie on the footbridge to find out what's just happened.

"You were very lucky today, Bob," my brother says.

"You've had a warning only this time, as it's the first time you've worn the Welsh Not. You won't get a second chance."

"Bob ..." says a voice behind me. "Bob ..."

It's Gwyneth. Her eyes are full of tears and she can't say anything else.

I nod to her and give her a little smile and then follow my brother up the path.

All night I think about my name being called at registration the next morning. That's what's in my head in bed and while I eat my porridge. That's all I can hear as I say 'cheerio' to Dad in bed and to Mam on the doorstep. That's what I talk to Owie about on the way to the village. That's why we're almost late and have to run across the yard to our lines or face the cane for arriving after nine o'clock.

As I take my seat next to Aled – thank the Lord, I say to myself – there's Eifiona sitting in front of me! She's better and she's here in school.

"He-urr-miss," she says when Mrs Barnwell calls her name.

I suddenly see lightning and worry even more. I'd settled with the idea that I'm going to get the Welsh Not for refusing to speak English again today, and I won't be able to escape the cane at the end of the afternoon this time.

"Roburrt Elees Jowns?"

I raise my hand in the air, as before.

"He-urr-miss." Eifiona's voice has spoken for me again.

Mrs Barnwell raises her eyes from the big book and says something about 'no need' and 'hand in thu ere' before going on to the next name. Aled grabs my arm and pulls it down.

I happen to look down the row and happen to meet Gwyneth's eye. She gives me the tiniest smile and then looks away.

I'm not sure what it is, but something happened in our little class that morning. I look over at Harri Big Mouth, as Aled calls him, and he's sitting low in his seat but there's no sign of strain on his face. Gwyneth holds her head up once more after the trouble yesterday.

Aled is by my side and Eifiona is in front of me.

Part 2

Llangernyw, March 1905

Chapter 1

I've just come home from Nain Bicycle's house. I read stories and articles in back copies of the *Cymru'r Plant* magazine every week and then I go to Nain's to discuss them every Saturday morning – that was her Christmas present to me. We've just been discussing Ogof Arthur – Arthur's Cave – and its treasures, and about the army that will awaken when Wales is ready to be led.

Mam wants me to go over the verse I will be reciting in the service to celebrate Saint David's Day in chapel tomorrow. I've learned it by heart and I practise it beside Dad's bed in the bedroom because he can't come to chapel tomorrow to hear me.

"Right, Bob; off you go," Mam says. "And loud enough so that everyone at the back can hear you clearly."

I clear my throat importantly and start to recite:

Dyrchafwn heddiw'n eon
Hen faner goch y ddraig
A mynnwn weld ei phlannu

Yng Nghymru ar bob craig;
Chwi fechgyn bryniau Gwalia,
Ymunwch o un fryd
I godi baner Cymru
Uwchlaw banerau'r byd.

"Very good, my lad," Dad says. "I've never heard that verse about raising our *hen faner goch y ddraig* above all other flags before. Our Jac says the Red Dragon flag, the flag of Wales, is the oldest flag in the world."

"Nain found it," I say, "in an old …"

"… in an old copy of *Cymru'r Plant*," says Mam with a smile. "That wasn't difficult to work out!"

"Did you bring one home with you today?" asks Dad. Nain lets me bring one copy home to read every week and then swap it for a new one the following Saturday. Jac helps me with my reading every weekend.

Dad wants to hear me 'read meaningfully', as he says. That means getting the words and sentences to flow naturally. I'm reading a piece about a magpie stealing a ring and hiding it in its nest. By the end of the piece Dad's in agony, having lain in the same position too long, and Mam has to give him a hand to turn slightly onto his side.

Dad hasn't moved from his bed since August and he doesn't seem to be getting better. We've had to go 'on the parish' because Dad can no longer work on the estate's farms. Mam had to go in front of the parish committee in the church, chaired by the vicar, and we receive five shillings a week. Since then Jac (who remains Jac Two-Trousers) has had to give up staying in lodgings in town and he borrows Nain Bicycle's bike to go to school in Llanrwst every day. Ifan brings a few shillings home every so often and no one asks where they've come from. I suspect they're something to do with the pheasant feathers and rabbit blood in our woodshed beyond our yard.

Owie is in the kitchen, with his nose in *Ystraeon o Hanes Cymru* by Owen M. Edwards, which tells stories from Welsh history. I ask him, "Do you have a story for me, Owie?"

"I'm looking in this for the bit about Dewi Sant – who we know now the English call Saint David – for tomorrow, but there's a good story here about Caradog," Owie says.

"Who was he, then?"

"He was a hero here in Wales when we were fighting the Romans," explains Owie. "In the end he was caught and they took him and his family all the way to Rome in chains to bow down in front of Caesar to plead for his life. Everyone bowed before Caesar, except Caradog. Listen to this:

'He was not afraid, though he was a prisoner. And everyone gazed at the king that had been so powerful, but was now in chains.'

Look – here's a picture of him. And he's saying to Caesar that he's a king himself, despite the fact that Rome is so strong and has taken so much of his land. And you know what? Caesar admired Caradog for being so brave and refusing to bow. He and his family were allowed to live in Rome for the rest of their days."

I'm looking at the picture. Caradog has long, untidy hair and a flowing beard. The illustration is in black and white, but if the beard were red he'd look similar to Mac, the Plas gamekeeper.

At the other end of the table Jac is surrounded by his books.

"Strange, isn't it, boys," says Jac. "I'm just reading Gibbon's *The History of the Decline and Fall of the Roman Empire* here. It's a history of the Roman empire crumbling. That's the story over and over in this world – big countries stealing from little countries, but the big countries fall to pieces in the end. I have Latin lessons in the school in Llanrwst – that was the Romans' language – and Latin was the language of the world at that time. But apart from school lessons it's a dead language today."

"Was there a Welsh Not when the Romans were in Wales, Jac?" I ask.

"No, the Romans didn't kill off the smaller languages." Jac says. "But many Welsh words we use have been borrowed from the Latin. Words like *pont* and *ffenest* and *eglwys* – the Romans gave us those."

"What is *pont* in English, Bob?" By now this is a game between Owie and me.

"Brij?"

"Yes. What about *ffenest*?"

"Windô."

"And *eglwys*?"

"Oh, I can't remember." And Owie reminds me.

"Pretty good, Bob," Jac says. "Caradog could speak Latin

with Caesar, I'm sure of that. Being able to speak another language can make you equal in rank ... if not stronger."

"But without losing your own language," Owie says.

"That's exactly what Owen Edwards says," Jac says. "And he's in a big college in Oxford and he's seen some of the wonders of Europe."

"Why aren't we allowed to speak Welsh in Ysgol y Llan, then?" I ask.

"It's an old way of thinking," Jac says, getting to his feet. He walks back and forth and I've never seen him fired up like this before. "Things are changing fast. Owen Edwards has written a book in Welsh about *our* – the native Welsh – history and he's been granted permission for it to be used in schools in Wales."

"I've seen pictures of classes of schoolchildren from Bangor, from Swansea, from the Rhondda Valley in *Cymru'r Plant*," I say. "They must read the magazine in school."

"Twelve thousand copies of *Cymru'r Plant* going to all parts of Wales and to some of the big towns in England every month," says Jac. "Dozens of schools now are starting to teach Welsh as a subject and teach Welsh history in Welsh."

"But not in Ysgol y Llan," says Owie.

"Ysgol y Llan is a Church School," explains Jac. "The vicar, Reverend Powell, does everything in English, the Colonel in the Plas goes to the church and does everything in English and Mr and Mrs Barnwell go to the church."

"So what's *eglwys* in English, Bob?" Owie asks playfully.
"Chyrch!"

"Yes," Jac says. "The Church of England is the 'church';

they're holding on tightly to the old ways. That's why we have the Welsh Not here in Llangernyw, but not in Pandy Tudur, which is only a couple of miles up the road."

"It's a pity we can't go to Ysgol Pandy Tudur, isn't it, Owie?" I say.

"Your father and I had no choice," says Mam, lifting her head from the pot on the fire. "Because your father gets so much work from the Plas estate and the church, we didn't have much choice when the vicar came to see us before any of you children started school."

"The Plas and the church own everything in the parish!" says Owie.

"Well, we're grateful to the parish now," says Mam, turning back to the dinner.

"Things are going to change," says Jac. "Lloyd George is in parliament and he's going to have a voice there. There's talk of an Education Department for Wales this year, and what's happening in the Sunday schools is going to lead to change in the day schools, you'll see. Books, teachers – that's what's needed now. Head teachers too – ones that can speak Welsh as well as English."

"Are you going to be a headmaster, Jac?" I ask.

"I'll be a teacher first, that's the way it's done," Jac explains. "But you're right – it's important for us to get new blood into schools in Wales and get a new generation of teachers that are willing to follow more open ideas, like those of Owen Edwards. That's what I'd like to do."

"Me too," says Owie softly. "I've not said a word about

this before, but that's what I'd like to do too – stand in front of a class and give the children a Welsh education. Think how wonderful that would be after what we've had!"

I turn all this over in my head until Mam's voice interrupts: "But education costs money, boys. It's no small thing to send someone to college – we're lucky to have Ifan and Betsi working and bringing a bit of money into this house, believe you me."

We're all quiet over dinner.

In the afternoon the three of us go out to work. Even though we don't have a smallholding, there is still plenty that needs doing: mucking out the henhouse and the pigsty, sweeping the yard, chopping firewood, and starting to dig the vegetable garden. Towards the end of the afternoon I'm in the woods collecting sticks for kindling when Fly the dog, playing around my heels, suddenly starts to growl.

"What's up, Fly *bach*?"

I crouch down to her and something makes me hide behind a gorse bush. I hear footsteps and I put my hands round Fly's throat and mouth so she doesn't make the slightest noise. Between the gorse prickles, I can see Mac the gamekeeper passing along the path. He has an opened gun in the crook of his folded left arm. From his right hand dangle two bloodied rabbits.

Once he's out of sight, I carry on collecting sticks until I've got a good bundle. On my way to the yard on the further side of Bronrhwylfa, I notice there are two rabbits hanging on our gate. There's no sign of Mac anywhere.

*   *   *

On Sunday afternoon, there's a very warm applause in the Saint David's Day celebration. The songs and poetry selections that are performed are splendid and I am filled with pride on hearing them all. I manage to remember every word of my verse and Mam, sitting at the back of the big vestry, smiles to show she's heard every word. Elen Jones comes over to us at the vestry door while everyone is having a cup of tea and a Welsh cake.

"A good piece, Bob. It was from *Cymru'r Plant*, wasn't it?" she asks me.

"Yes, Elen Jones," I answer in surprise. "Do you read it too?"

"I get it every month."

"When will we get it in school?" I ask her.

"This lad's got a good voice in chapel," says Elen Jones to Mam, changing the subject. "But you know what, Lisa Jones, he's like a little mouse in school."

"He must be shy," Mam says. "I was the same."

"Yes, maybe," Elen Jones says. "But the school inspectors are visiting next week and they'll want to hear every child reading and answering. The school has been waiting for a long time for him to find his voice – but he has no choice but to try his very best next week."

Jac is listening to the conversation. After Elen Jones has moved on to another family, he takes hold of my arm.

"It's that school that's at fault. That place suffocates you, Bob."

Chapter 2

As I walk down the path towards the footbridge with Owie that Monday morning, I see a magpie fly towards the ancient yew tree in the churchyard and disappear among its dark branches. The magpie is easy to identify from the picture in *Cymru'r Plant* because its feathers are black and white, exactly the same as the ink on the paper of the magazine.

"I'm sure there's a magpie's nest in the old yew, Owie," I say to him.

"Get a move on, Bob. We haven't got time to go looking for birds' eggs this morning."

Reverend Powell is in the school that morning. He leads the prayers and then gives a speech in front of all the classes together. I only understand the odd word, but at home that night Owie tells me that he'd said he wants us to do our best during the inspectors' visit on Wednesday, for the good name of the school. I ask Owie what will happen when they come.

"They're men who work for the state education office," explains Owie. "They come to see the work of every school once a year to make sure the children are being taught properly and that the standard of work and state of the building are alright. They'll talk to the teachers and the assistants and see the older classes' books, and then listen to the children read and ask questions."

"What sort of questions?"

"They asked me 'What poetry do you know?' once."

"What's that?"

"Verses that you've learned by heart, you know?"

"Could I recite the *faner goch y ddraig* verse, Owie?"

"No, it would have to be something in English, Bob."

"What, like that stupid 'lickle lam' thing? That's not up to much."

"But that's what they'll want to hear. Can you remember it?"

"Meh-ri ada lickle lam,
Lickle lam, lickle lam,
Meh-ri ada lickle lam,
Its flees as whyt as snô."

"Very good, Bob. Can you say that in school?"

"But I've got no voice in school, Owie."

"Is that no better?"

"No, Owie. Jac says it's the shock of seeing you caned on the first day. He remembers feeling something similar when he saw a girl getting the cane for speaking Welsh in the playground – but that was about a month after he started school, and it only lasted a morning for him. Some children – and adults – get a stammer from having a shock or something horrible happen to them. But some – like me – can't speak at all in some places."

"What's strange is that you know plenty of the words by now – you say them to yourself inside, but no one outside can hear you."

"I'm like that bat that was in Nain Bicycle's house, aren't I

– making a noise that no one else can hear."

"But you heard it, Bob?"

"I did. I read in *Cymru'r Plant* that the bats will be coming out of hibernation this month, if it warms up. I wonder if it'll come back to Nain's house."

"Spring's ahead of us, as Dad always says," says Owie.

*   *   *

On Wednesday morning, I see the magpie disappear into the yew again on the way to school. I wonder if it'll bring me luck.

The inspector is in the classroom as we walk to our desks.

We have all been instructed to wash our hand and not to dirty our clothes on the way to school. Everyone is orderly and totally quiet. There's a large stone in my stomach today.

After registration and prayers, we get the second verse in the babies' class to copy onto our slates from the blackboard. More of the story of Mary and her 'lickle lam':

> He followed her to school one day,
> School one day, school one day,
> He followed her to school one day
> Which was against the rule.
> It made the children laugh and play,
> Laugh and play, laugh and play,
> It made the children laugh and play
> To see the lamb in school.

This takes ages as we've been warned to make every letter tidy and every line straight. While we're hard at work, one of the two inspectors walks along the rows between the desks and looks at our slates over our shoulders. He points at Aled's slate:

"How do you say that word?"

"Fol ... fol-ow-d, sir."

"Very good. And what does it mean?"

"Go by her back, sir."

"Yes. Very good. Carry on."

He's looking over my shoulder now and I can feel his breath on the back of my neck. The sides of my throat have met in the middle.

"Very tidy, boy. Very tidy lettering. Would you 'laugh and play' if a lamb came to school?"

I turn my face towards him with a big smile, and nod my head. I've understood the question. I smile still wider and mouth 'I-ess, sir' and the inspector goes on: "Yes, it would make everybody want to laugh and play wouldn't it? Carry on. Good work."

And he goes on to the next child. Poor Glyn doesn't understand his question. Neither do most of the girls in the front row. I'm breathing quickly. But I think everything is all right. I sense Mrs Barnwell's eyes boring through the glass of her spectacles as she stares at me.

*   *   *

After playtime, the inspectors look at the register and then listen to us say our numbers. The man looking at our class asks some of the girls to name figures on their own.

After dinner, they walk round the yard and the toilets and

look at the walls and ceiling inside the school. They both have little books and they've been writing notes in them all day. They listen to us singing, and their heads nod and they exchange a smile during that lesson. As the end of the afternoon approaches the older inspector says that they're going to ask one from each class to come forward and recite poetry in front of the whole school.

He picks Nel from the top class and she starts to recite 'The Lady of the Lake'. But she can't get further than six lines. Then John from Owie's class recites two verses of 'The Beggarman'. From Miss Elen's class, it's Gwenda who's chosen to recite 'The Little Brown Bird'. Then the other inspector stands in front of our class. He looks from face to face ...

"And you, the young chap with the tidy handwriting, you come and say the first verse of 'Mary had a little lamb', will you?"

"On your feet!" says Mrs Barnwell.

I stand up. I walk to the end of the row and stand in front of the class.

"Right, young man. When you are ready."

I open my mouth but I know that no sound is going to come out of it. I mouth the first line.

"I can't hear you, boy."

I carry on mouthing.

"Louder!"

And that's when Mrs Barnwell intervenes.

"He has had a severe cold recently – lost his voice and it's gone again today. Hm ... I'm sure he could write it all out from memory for you if you wish."

"No, no. That won't be necessary."

I return to my seat and keep my head down until I'm out of the playground and running across the footbridge at the end of the afternoon.

As I wait for Owie there, I see the magpie – I'm sure it's the same one – on the branch of a tree on the boundary of the churchyard.

"Look at that magpie over there, Aled," I say. "It's looking for treasure, guaranteed."

"What d'you mean, Bob? What treasure?" asks Aled.

"Treasure?" say Gwyneth and Eifiona and pause for a second. "Do you know where there's treasure?"

"That magpie over there knows where there's some," I say, starting to enjoy the story. "There's a magpie's nest in the old, old yew tree in the churchyard. Magpies hoard sparkling treasures to decorate their nests and if that yew is four thousand years old, I'm sure there's tons of treasure in the nest."

"Four thousand years old?" Some of the older lads have stopped to listen now.

"What's the name of this river?" I ask the gang beside the bridge.

"Collen," says Aled. "I know that because you told me once before. It's the same name as the hazel tree."

"There was once a young lad who cut a hazel stick in those woods over there so he could drive two bullocks to Llanrwst fair." I recall one of the stories from *Cymru'r Plant* now and relocating it to Llangernyw makes it more real, somehow.

"In the fair, an old man comes up to him and carefully studies the stick. 'Where did you get this?' he asks the lad. 'Coed Rhan Hir,' he replies. 'Take me to the place.' They walk all the way to Llangernyw and the lad shows him the exact hazel tree from where he cut his stick. 'Go home and get me a spade,' says the old man. When the lad comes back with the spade, the old man digs a hole under the hazel's roots and there he reveals a large cave full of treasure. And I wouldn't be surprised if there's not a fair bit of that gold and silver in that magpie's nest over there!"

"Is that an old story, Bob?" Eifiona asks.

"No, it's a new old story," I say.

"Come on home, you clown." That's Owie.

We climb the path towards the road together.

* * *

The next morning, it's the lines in the playground and then into class. Somehow, I've foreseen what unfolds as if it's already happened.

I'm not in the least surprised when Mr Barnwell comes across from his class and stands in front of ours.

His cane is in his hands.

He points the tip at me.

I get up and step to the end of the row and then walk up to the headmaster.

"Right hand out."

I hold out my right hand and turn my head away from the rows of desks.

"For refusing to speak English," Mr Barnwell says. Whap. My hand feels as if I've got hold of a hot poker.

"Left hand out."

"For refusing to speak English," he says, followed by another whap. "Go back to your seat, boy, and don't be insolent in class ever again."

I walk back to my seat with tears running down my cheeks.

But as I do so, something strange happens inside me. The stone in my stomach is lighter now. I feel the dry rope that binds my guts slacken and my throat starts to open, even.

Mrs Barnwell is calling the girls' names.

"He-urr-miss ...He-urr-miss ..."

She starts to call the boys' names and when she gets to 'Roburrt Elees Jowns?' I open my mouth before Eifiona can answer for me and say clearly: "He-urr-miss!"

I'm here. This is how it'll be for now. But tomorrow's another day.

Chapter 3

As we come to the edge of Coed Twlc on the way home, we see that Dei Coch is in the ditch, busy with his pickaxe and square spade. Beside him is Mac the gamekeeper; the two redheads are deep in conversation and don't hear us until we are right beside them.

"Good afternoon to you, you brainy scholars!" says Dei Coch when he eventually notices us.

He goes on to ask after Dad's health and we answer him. Then he turns to the keeper, who is still standing in the road beside the ditch.

"You know Donald MacDonald the keeper, don't you?"

"Yes Dei," answers Owie. "We've been beating for his grouse shoot on Mynydd Moelogan."

Mac says something I can't understand.

"Mac is asking if you were good boys in school today," translates Dei Coch.

"Well, Bob got the cane, didn't he," Owie replies.

"Good gracious me, what for, Bob *bach*?"

"For not speaking English," I say.

"Look, the marks from the cane are still there," says Owie, catching hold of my hands and showing my palms to the men.

"Oh, those look nasty, Bob," Dei says, before turning to Mac and telling him what's happened. I catch the words 'Welsh Not' in Dei's explanation.

"Ach, Sassenachs," Mac says angrily, spitting into the ditch. I remember that it's his word for the English. Then he tells Dei Coch some story, which Dei Coch relays to us in Welsh.

"You know that Donald comes from the Isle of Skye in the north of Scotland, don't you? When he went to infants' school on the island, he, too, was punished for speaking his own language. The language of the island people is Gaelic – it's a language that was related to Welsh before the time of the Romans, he says. What the schoolteacher did in Scotland was to put the head of a dead fox on the head of the child who had spoken Gaelic and then whoever was wearing it at the end of the day got the cane."

"The same as with our Welsh Not!" Owie says.

"How awful!" I say. "Some old disgusting, stinky head of a fox on a little child's head!"

"Yes, awful, Mac?" Dei Coch turns to the gamekeeper and raises his voice. "*Pen llwynog* – fox's head! *Cansen* – cane!"

"Ach, *pen llwynog* – yess, Dei," Mac answers. "And I couldn't *siarad yn iawn* afterwards. Stutter. What's that in Welsh, Dei?"

"*Atal deud*, Mac – you had *atal deud*?"

"Och, yess," Mac says. "Bad *iawn*. Very *drwg*. And it came back during the war, you rememberr, Dei?"

"Yes, I do, now you come to mention it," Dei Coch says.

Mac can speak Welsh! I've never heard a word of Welsh from him before.

"Yess! *Pen llwynog. Cansen!*" he says then, miming the stick hitting his hand.

"*Ew*, can Mac speak Welsh?" asks Owie.

"A little, eh, Mac?" says Dei. "*Cymraeg tipyn bach*?"

"Yess. *Cymraeg tipyn bach* goes a long way," says the Scotsman. "It's a stupid hen that listens to Mister Llwynog!"

"How did he learn Welsh?" Owie asks.

"Mac and I were in the Boer War in South Africa until a couple of years ago," Dei says. "He was a soldier in the Scots Fusiliers and I was in the Welch Fusiliers. We were in some of the same battles in Transvaal and the Orange Free State."

"Do you have to have red hair before you can join the army, Dei?" I ask, looking at the two ex-soldiers together.

Dei translates this for Mac and they both double up laughing. This is the first time I've seen Mac smile, let alone laugh.

"*Y lemon gwirion*, Mac," Dei says, pointing at me.

"Yess, *lemon gwirion*, Dei!" says the gamekeeper.

"No, I'm a Welshman and Mac's a Scot," explains Dei. "When the Sassenachs – as Mac would call them – say they want to go to war they make sure that there's plenty of Welsh and Scots in the front line, eh, Mac?"

"Yess," he nods, having heard 'Sassenachs' and 'front line', "Sassenachs!"

"Give your dad our regards," Dei calls after us as we leave.

After arriving home at Bronrhwylfa, I have to repeat the story of the punishment to Mam and Dad, and show them the red weals on the palms of my hands.

There's a long silence in the bedroom, then Dad moves uncomfortably in his bed and says: "Well, Lisa, they've all had it now. Every one of the children we've brought up has been caned at some point for speaking Welsh in school."

"We can't do anything about it," Mam says.

"That's the worst of it, nothing is what we can do," says Dad, before turning to me. "You'd better go and tell your *nain* your story."

Nain Bicycle reaches for a copy of *Cymru'r Plant* on hearing what's happened.

"I've just got the March issue in Llanrwst fair, see here, Bob. Owen Edwards always says in his message to the children that people that can read about their country's history and heroes in their own language are enriched. He goes on to say that schools in Wales are improving every year, that things are better than they were when your mam and your dad were in school, and that there's a new spirit in the land. This is what's on the first page of this issue, look:

.

'The most valuable treasure that Wales has is its language. There was a time when it was regarded as worthless, and worse than worthless; and it was discredited and disrespected and distained. But today it's value is a recognised; and very soon there will not be a school left in Wales that does not teach Welsh.'"

"But Nain, I'm in Ysgol y Llan – and there's not a word of Welsh there! And worse still, we get the cane for saying a word in Welsh."

"What *Cymru'r Plant* is saying is that there's a change afoot," Nain says. "All this that you've got to bear now won't be here for much longer. The old ways haven't worked, Owen

Edwards says, because if you try to force words on children that don't mean anything to them, they don't learn them. Education has to appeal to the mind and to the soul – and a the moment Ysgol y Llan does neither of these."

"So how's that going to change?"

"Take Jac. He's chosen his path," says Nain.

"What path is that, Nain?"

"The way of the fox, some call it," Nain says, a mischievous smile playing on her lips. "He's taken what he got from Ysgol y Llan – yes, the cane, but the words too. He passed the scholarship to get a free education a Llanrwst County School."

"But that's an English school as well, Jac says!" I say. "None of the teachers speak Welsh with him. There's more Latin there than Welsh."

"I know that," concedes Nain, "but that's another step on the path too. He'll be in college in Bangor next year, you can be sure of that. Another step. And do you know what he's going to do then?"

"He's going to be a teacher, Nain!" I say. "He'll be a teacher, waving his cane and sticking the Welsh Not round schoolchildren's necks!"

"Well, of course he won't do that!" Nain says. "Don't you remember what I said about the 'way of the fox'? There are some stone walls that are too high for the fox to jump when he's running from the hunt. But he doesn't lose heart. Some people have seen the fox jump and kick the top stones of a wall. When those stones fall on either side of the wall, those stones'll make it a little easier for him to jump the wall – and jump back. The walls of Ysgol y Llan are an obstacle – you and Owie are right in the middle of that now. Jac has jumped over that obstacle and when he becomes a teacher, he won't be following the old way of teaching. The children of Wales today will be the teachers and leaders of tomorrow's Wales – and this country will be a much better place by then."

Nain places three more pieces of peat on the fire and they give off blue smoke.

"Peat for the fire, d'you see," she says, suddenly turning towards me. "Peat from Rhos-y-mawn, the other side of Coed Twlc, this is. What better than peat from our own land to give us heat and light. C'mon!"

She stands up and flings on a coat and scarf and walks out to the road.

"The days are getting longer, Bob," she tells me. "Let's go towards the sunlight."

We are heading straight up the road, past Penffordd-deg, Bron yr Haul and Bodunig. Nain names the fields closest to me and the farms on the further slopes: Llwyn Du, Tŷ Gwyn and Nant-erw. Then she does the same with the higher hills – Tre-pys-llygod above Llangernyw, then Moel Unben; Moel Derwydd and Moel Gydia above Gwytherin; Mynydd Moelogan and Rhos-y-mawn and Foel Gadeiriau behind us. The names rattle off her tongue.

"I'm walking a lot more these days, Bob," she says. "Now that Jac has my bike to go to Llanrwst every day, I'm Nain No-Bicycle, aren't I! These names are great company to me as I walk. Here we are above Wenlli now, see. And what a view!"

She isn't wrong. We both stand and gaze at the orange sky

before us. Against the sunset are the peaks of huge, bare mountains, standing dark and mysterious. Nain knows the names of them all.

"We'll start by the sea over there, to the right. You've got Tal y Fan, Drum, Foel Fras, Foel Grach, Carnedd Llywelyn, Penllithrig-y-wrach Carnedd Dafydd, Pen yr Helgi Du, Tryfan and Moel Siabod. Then the Carneddau and the Glyderau – these are some of the highest mountains in Eryri, Bob, or in 'Snowdonia' as the English have it. These have protected the Welsh down the centuries and they still stand with us today. I feel a sort of strength in my backbone when I look at this view."

The pair of us watch the orange light turn to dark orange and the mountains darken. Behind us the night sky is spreading.

"Come on, Bob, or the night will catch us out."

On the way home, I wonder if seeing the mountains might improve Dad's back.

Chapter 4

"Tell me now, Owie," I say over my porridge on Monday morning, "what's the meaning of this word 'he-urr' – is it 'listen' or what?"

"'He-urr mee now' – that's 'listen', Bob," says Owie. "But 'he-ur is thu *uwd*', that's 'here is the porridge'."

"Goodness, this English is really confusing, Owie! Eifiona said it was 'listen' and Aled said it was 'here'."

"So what will you say when you say 'He-urr-miss' to Mrs Barnwell this morning?" asks Owie.

"Here I am, miss,
And there's the floor.
And there's the *sgwlyn*
On a see-saw!"

"You be careful you do no such thing, Bob!" Mam shouts from Dad's bedside.

"Cheerio, Mam! Cheerio, Dad!" Out the door we go.

*   *   *

"He-urr-miss!" Every syllable bursts so clearly from my lips as I answer the register for Mrs Barnwell. So much so that Eifiona and Gwyneth half turn to look at me and smile.

"Sit still. No turning round in class!" snaps Mrs Barnwell.

After we've finished with the register and praying, the headmaster calls for the attention of the whole school. He has a mouthful of big words.

"Pronunciation, children. It is very, very important," says Mr Barnwell. "We noticed that it was very poor for the inspectors last week. We have received their report – it is not very good."

He turns to look at our class and quotes from the report in front of him:

"The infants were very backward."

He turns to the rest of the school and reads:

"The great prevalence of Welsh may be received to some degree as an excuse for the present unsatisfactory state of this school. A more systematic effort should be made to teach the children English."

He puts the report down and asks quietly:

"What is the name of this school, children?" And then he shouts: "And two strokes of the cane to anyone who says 'Ysgol y Llan'!"

Gillian Davies puts up her hand.

"Llangernyw School, sir," she says smugly.

"No," says the headmaster curtly. "Tell them please, Mrs Barnwell."

"The Church of England School, Llangerniew," she says, pronouncing our village name as 'Lan-gurn-yew'.

"How do we say 'Llangerniew'?" questions Mr Barnwell.

"Lan-gurn-yew," the school replies.

We have a full three minutes of practice to pronounce it the same way as the Plas family and the Reverend Powell do.

That week, the Welsh Not is used every day, with a caning at the end of each afternoon.

"It seems to answer the purpose," the headmaster says.

*   *   *

A pleasant surprise awaits Owie and I when we get home from school on Thursday afternoon. Dad is up and sitting at the kitchen table to have tea with us.

"Dad!" I exclaim, and run towards him.

"Steady on, Bob!" Mam shouts. "Don't jump on his knee or anything like that!"

I instantly freeze, but Dad ruffles my hair with his right hand, while still supporting the base of his back with his left.

"One step at a time, lads, that's the way," Dad says. "But it's great to get out of bed, I can tell you that."

"Did you get some new medicine from the doctor, or something, Dad?" Owie asks.

"No," Mam answers for him. "Did you notice how warm it was this afternoon. It's like the first day of spring."

We look behind us and notice that Mam has the outside door open. It faces the afternoon sun and there's a sort of golden glow on the landscape laid out under a blue sky.

"We saw daffodils beside the river Collen," I say. "I'm sure they were the small Welsh ones. It says somewhere in the *Cymru'r Plant* that small daffodils with double petals are the Welsh ones."

"They bloom later than garden daffodils," Dad says. "And

that reminds me. It's high time we started digging the potato patch in the garden so we can get them planted before the end of March. Is there a good load of last year's pig manure in the compost heap, Owie?"

"Yes, Dad. I can start shifting it with the wheelbarrow after tea."

"And what about the seed potatoes, Bob? Did you put them under newspaper on the shelves in the far shed?"

"Yes, Dad. I had a peep at them last Saturday. Some have sprouted quite long shoots by now."

"Well, off you go to do the trenches, then, lads. Jac finished the digging last weekend."

My jam sandwich tastes all the sweeter for having Dad at the tea table, talking about the garden.

*   *   *

Owie is struggling with a wheelbarrow full of stinking pig manure when Dad comes to lean on the frame of the back door to see how we're doing.

"This row's as crooked as a dog's hind leg!" he shouts at me. I've been at it for a quarter of an hour, trying to dig a trough with a spade so that the manure can go in the bottom of it before planting the vegetables. I've tried to remember how Dad did it last spring. Face the trench, spade into the soil and push it right in with my heel, step back and lift the soil to the left. Then a step back and do the same again. The problem is I lose my direction when I step back and the row is all over the place.

"You need a bit of twine," says Dad, trying to cross the yard towards us. "You'll find some in the drawer in the far shed."

But he has to stand still. Both hands are at his back and he's in pain again. Who should happen to pass at that moment but Dei Coch and Mac.

"Steady on, Wil Jones!" shouts Dei Coch. "Hold on. We'll be with you now."

The two men support Dad by his armpits. After hearing what we're trying to do, Dei Coch tells me: "Run to the kitchen and bring a chair for your dad. A bit of fresh air will do him no end of good. We'll sit him down in the yard at the end of this row and he can keep an eye on you."

Off I go to the kitchen and bring back Dad's favourite chair, the one with the tall back and wooden arms. As I start to cross the yard, Mac comes over and lifts the chair from my grasp.

After setting Dad in his place, Mac says something to Dei.

"Well, yes; Mac here's had a good idea," Dei says to Dad. "What d'you think of this, Wil? There's a lot needs doing in the Plas gardens now that spring's on the way. What if Mac were to ask the head gardener if these two could go there to work every Saturday? They'd get a shilling a day."

"A shilling a day!" yells Owie, almost losing control of the wheelbarrow and tipping the load of manure onto the yard.

"Ha!" laughs Mac. "Look at that *hogyn* and his *berfa*!"

"How many words of Welsh does Mac know?"

"There are a few Welsh words that are the same in Gaelic," Dei says.

"*Tarw!*" says Mac, making a bull's horns on his head with his fingers.

Fly appears from somewhere, wagging her tail.

"*Tyrd yma* – come here, good girl," the gamekeeper calls to her, fussing her when she comes to him. "Good Scots dog! Border collie."

"Did you know our sheepdogs are dogs from *yr Alban*, Bob?" Dad says.

"Alba – *da iawn*! Dog from Alba – very good," says Mac.

"Alba in Gaelic is what we call *yr Alban* in Welsh," explains Dei Coch. "Take him to see the pigs, Bob."

Mac comes over to the pigsty with me. The piglets have all been slaughtered at the start of last winter but the two sows are both ready to give birth to new litters of piglets this spring.

"Ha! *Mochyn*," says Mac on seeing them.

"No – *hwch*," I say, pointing at their teats.

"*Dau hwch*," Mac offers, holding up two fingers.

"*Dwy hwch*," I correct him.

"*Un hwch tenau ac un hwch tew*," Mac ventures; "One thin sow and one fat sow," he repeats to himself in English.

"One thin sow

And one fat sow,

A little dog from Scotland

And pussy says 'miaow'!" I rhyme in Welsh.

Mac laughs all the way back to the vegetable garden. Before leaving, he says a line of something to Dei Coch and he nods and says: "Amen to that".

"What did he say, Dei?" asks Dad.

"It's an old proverb from Scotland that came to his mind, Wil, after seeing the lovely manure you have here: 'A good muck heap is the mother of a Sunday dinner!' True enough, isn't it?"

*   *   *

Eventually, Friday afternoon comes around. The school bell. On the other side of the footbridge, Owie's waiting for me. He has two of his friends with him and, as Aled and I cross towards them, one of them calls to me with a smile:

"Here he is, Bob the Story! Have you got some tale to tell us today?"

Eifiona and Gwyneth are behind me and in no time quite a gang had gathered. I quickly wrack my brains and then remember the mountains Nain had named last night.

"You see that mountain over there, the other side of the bridge," I say. "Do you know its name?"

Silence. No one's ever heard of it and I silently thank Nain Bicycle.

"It's called Tre-pys-llygod and there's a good story behind the name."

"Don't want to hear it," says Gillian Davies in English, passing by with her nose in the air. "No use to me at all. No use!"

She doesn't speak Welsh to anyone now. She says 'no use at all!' every time she hears the language and makes an effort to speak English with everyone everywhere. She's given up going to chapel and has now joined the church.

"No yoose!" says Harri *bach* then, dodging past us up the path with his new friend from the Bridge Inn.

"Get lost, Harri *bach*," shouts one of the big boys.

"Mai nêm iss Henry, not Harri," he shouts, and then turns round and pulls a face when he's far enough away.

"A giant lived on top of that mountain in the olden days," I start my story. "This is a new story so you have to be quiet because I've got to make it up and say it at the same time! The giant was very fond of cheese and he would go to the Market Hall in Llanrwst every Tuesday for the market and every Wednesday for the fair, and buy all the cheese from the stalls there and then carry it home to the top of that mountain over there. He was a very big giant – it only took him ten steps for him to go from Llangernyw to Llanrwst.

"Because of all the truckles of cheese he bought in Llanrwst, he needed huts to keep them in. Every week, the giant would build a circular hut, then go to Llanrwst and fill the hut and close the door. He kept enough cheese on his own table to last the week. During the week, he'd build another hut, go down to the Market Hall and fill it up, and so on, and so on.

"By the end of the summer he had fifteen huts full of cheese on top of the mountain. The Llangernyw people called the mountain 'cheese-town' at the time – Tre-caws.

"But when September arrived, the weather started to grow cold. As you all know, the little field mice move into the walls of houses around that time of year. One little mouse went through the wall of one of the cheese huts on the summit of the mountain ... and she thought she'd gone to heaven! She ate and ate the cheese all day until she was strong enough to open the door and go and tell her family and friends about it.

"All the mice of Llangernyw went to the top of the mountain to eat cheese that night. They ate and ate throughout September. In October, the giant came home from Llanrwst fair very sad. There was no cheese to be had – the grazing was poor in the valley and there would be no cheese until the next summer. But suddenly he remembered the cheese in the huts.

"'Hooray!' he said, 'I've got enough cheese to last me through the winter.' But when he opened the first hut, there was no cheese there, only a pile of poo – you know the little round poos you see in the house sometimes: mouse peas!

"He opens the door of every hut. The only things left in them were mouse peas. And ever since then, the name of that mountain over there has been 'mouse-peas-town' – Tre-pys-llygod!"

"Hooray!" cried one of the girls, and claps her hands.

"And there's a song," I say then. "It goes like this:

Giant with his cheese,
Stores it with ease.
Mousey says 'yes, please' –
Nothing left but peas!"

We bellow this song out over and over as we make our way up the path, deafening the whole village.

Chapter 5

Getting out of bed was no problem that Saturday morning. By eight o'clock, Owie and I had devoured our porridge and a crust of toast each, and arrived at the garden through Coed y Plas.

Even arriving within the grounds of the Plas through the back door, so to speak, we realised we'd arrived in a place very different from the houses and farmhouses and land that we were familiar with. There are roads leading through areas of tidy grass, which are not bounded by hedges or fences and are free of animals. Here and there are single trees, tall and with their branches spread wide around them. Even the trees are different to the ones we are used to. Between the trees, as we get closer to the house, large evergreen bushes are coming into flower – once again the flowers are much larger than those we'd see on a blackthorn or an apple tree.

In the distance, we are able to see the back of the Plas itself, with its grand walls at different angles, and its slate roof and tall chimneys. To the left there is a tall wall with a wooden door. This is the wall of the vegetable garden.

"This is the door we're supposed to go through, Bob," Owie says. "That's what Dei Coch said – then look for Ben Lloyd, the head gardener."

"*Ew*, look at all the smoke coming from the chimneys," I say. "I'd say there must be a fire in every room in the Plas."

"Come on; don't dawdle."

Opening the door was like stepping into yet another world. Footpaths for the workers criss-crossing at right angles between the beds of earth. Along the walls there were fruit trees, pruned and pegged into special shapes. The soft fruit bushes – the blackcurrants and gooseberries – are grouped together. I recognise leeks growing in another bed, but most of the beds are bare, except the odd strip covered in straw.

Two of the workers are carrying wooden stakes and marking out a path with them on part of the soil furthest from us. Just then I see short man wearing a hat, brown corduroy trousers and a blue canvas jacket coming towards us.

"Hello, lads. I'm Ben Lloyd. I'll be looking after you here," he says. He adds, with a mischievous sparkle in his eyes, "And making sure that you have enough work to do. You see that row of red brick sheds over there? Come with me and we'll leave your coats and your packed lunch there."

It is a workers' hut. There is a wooden table and half a dozen or so chairs, some with jackets over them already. We leave our coats and our bag of food.

"You've done a bit of gardening already, Mac tells me," Ben Lloyd says.

"I weeded turnips for about a month last summer," Owie answers.

"That's hard work," said the gardener. "On all fours all day scrabbling in the soil, the rows long and too many of them!"

"Yes, that's it to a T," smiles Owie.

"Well, that's not the sort of gardening that we do here at the Plas," Ben says. "Your dad's got a bit of a garden, hasn't he, and you've been giving him a helping hand?"

"We've planted peas and beans this week," I say.

"In straight rows?" Ben asks.

"They're alright, I'd say," says Owie.

"Well, the way this garden looks is as important as the flavour of the produce, you know," says the gardener. It's too early for weeds, but there's enough work clearing, preparing, digging rows – straight ones – and starting to dig. Come with me to get the tools."

We had never seen such a collection of forks, spades, shovels, rakes, sickles, shears, wheelbarrows, pickaxes, saws and all sorts of other strange equipment before.

"A fork each and a wheelbarrow," Ben says, and we set about finding tools that suit our size. "You'd better have a rake too. Come with me."

Ben Lloyd leads us through a wooden door in the furthest wall of the garden and we come to a row of glasshouses with the morning sun on their glass fronts and the wall's stonework as their back wall.

"These face south, you see. Enough sun, but enough shelter from those trees over there as well. Even though they're a bit of a way off, they keep the wind and storms at bay."

"What grows in these, Ben Lloyd?" Owie asks.

"Grapes, peaches, lemons, all sorts of fruit from hot countries – and also tomatoes, peppers and the like. Just now some of the trees have been pruned, ready for new growth – the branches all need carrying to the compost heap over there, by the edge of the woods. Rake up the old, dry leaves and twigs that are lying about the place and then fork them up."

Ben Lloyd unlocks the door and leaves the key in the lock.

"We have to lock this so that light fingers can't nick the expensive fruit here," the gardener says.

"Little mousey fingers, do you mean?" I ask, thinking back to my Tre-pys-llygod story.

"Well, there's some pretty big beasts with light fingers too," laughs Ben Lloyd.

It's a beautiful morning and there's enough work to keep us busy. I carry the largest branches out and rake all the little bits into pile, and Owie wheels the barrow back and forth.

At about midday, who do I see coming out of the woods with his gun laid across his arm but Mac. He's having a word with Owie, who's emptying another wheelbarrow load onto the compost heap. He bends down and lifts a few twigs onto the heap and tidies round its base, and then walks over the open ground to the glasshouse where I've started to fork the next load by now.

"*Borrre da!*" says Mac. He always says three 'r's' where we'd say one.

"Goot morning!" I say back, with a small smile.

"Ha! You learn Sassenach, I learn Cymraeg," he says kindly.

"*Fforch*," I say.

"Fork," he says. "Very similar. Glass."

He taps the window of the building.

"*Gwydr*," I say.

"*Gwydrrr*. House?" he says, gesturing towards the roof and walls around us.

"*Tŷ*," I say.

"*Tŷ gwydrrr*," Mac says.

"House glass," I say.

"Yess, but we say 'glass-house' in English," Mac explains.

Mac goes on to name something else but a movement at the edge of the woods catches my eye. As Owie is now on his way back towards the glasshouse with the empty wheelbarrow, and Mac's back is towards the glass, only I see what's there. I see Ifan my brother. He's come out of the trees suddenly and looks as if he's lost. All I know is that he doesn't want Mac to see him. What shall I do?

Suddenly, unable to think of anything else, I run out through the door, close it behind me, lock it, take the key out of the lock and show it to Mac through the glass.

"*Goriad*," I say, when I've got his attention.

"Open the doorr, you little monkey!" is Mac's response.

"*Goriad. GOR-IAD!*" I say.

"Open it!"

"Ôp-en it." I play up, imitating Mac. Mac's face gradually turns the same colour as his hair. The dry skin across his cheek and down to the base of his nape turns purple and yellow.

"No, no – that's a key. Put it in the door and let me out."

"*Ci*," I tease. "*Ci* is dog?"

"No, key is – what you call it." The gamekeeper is yelling

at the top of his voice by now. "Aaa! Arrrrr! Let me OUT!"

"*Goriad*," I say.

"*Gorrriad*," Mac says. "Put the gorrr ... a what is it? Put the dog in the door and ..."

The keeper has completely lost it by now. His red hair is dripping with sweat and every muscle in his face is pulsating.

I've never seen anyone's face distorted in such fury before – not even Mr Barnwell when he's caning one of the children.

I realise I can't push him any further. Without looking at his face, I push the key back into the keyhole. But my fingers are sweaty and awkward and maybe the lock is a little stiff after the winter. I completely fail to turn the key to unlock the door.

"Op... op... open it! L... L... Let me out! F... F... fire!" Mac roars through his stammer. He's going mad in his glass prison and pounding on the windows with his two huge, hard fists. Fire? *Tân*? I don't understand ...

I give the key another try, but it's too stiff for me.

"S... S... Stand back!" orders Mac.

With the butt of his gun, he breaks one of the panes of glass in the door – the one nearest the lock. Wildly, he reaches through the broken pane and gets hold of the key. As he turns it I see blood running down his arm. Then he pulls his arm back in, turns the door handle and walks free from his prison.

He passes me like a whirlwind, as if I weren't there, with his gun on his shoulder by now.

"What's going on here?" Owie has reached me and is looking at me, confused, as he sees Mac making off, completely out of control. By looking over Owie's shoulder, I see that the noisy drama has sent Ifan back into the woods and that it's safe to let the keeper out of his trap.

"I was trying to teach the work '*goriad*' to him," I say. "But I think he'd had enough of his lessons."

*   *   *

When we arrive home after a long day in the Plas garden, we both put the shilling's wage we've received on the dresser for Mam. I can't help noticing that there are three more shillings on the dresser already.

"Was Ifan here today, Mam?" I ask in an innocent voice.

"Yes, he popped in at the end of the afternoon," is the answer.

Chapter 6

Later that night, I'm chatting with Nain about items in *Cymru'r Plant*. We're looking at signs of spring in the nature column and Jac is there to teach the odd word of English every now and again.

"People with two languages have twice as much to offer," says Jac. "Remember about the way of the fox again – you learn two languages and it'll be easier for you to get a job. Before too long being able to speak Welsh will be a great asset to do most of the public service jobs in our country."

There's an unexpected knock at the door. When Nain comes back into the kitchen, she brings the visitor with her. I panic slightly on seeing the shock of red hair and thick beard. I wasn't expecting to see the keeper here in Nain's house. To be honest, I wasn't keen on seeing him for quite a while.

"Mac is here to ask after you," says Nain Bicycle. "He called at Bronrhwylfa and heard you were here."

Jac greets him in English and is surprised to hear him say the odd word in Welsh and point at me, saying it's the 'young laddie' who's been teaching him. After Mac has said his piece, Jac turns to me and says: "Something's worrying Donald, Bob. He shouted at you today and he regrets it. He's come here to apologise and to explain why he behaved that way by telling you his story. That is, if you're willing for him to tell it and me to translate for you."

I'm looking at Mac's arm and I can see a pretty bad cut where the glass from the door had stabbed him. He's washed the wound but there's still a clear scab on his skin. The dry skin on half his face is still very red as well.

"Yes, of course," I say, looking at his injury and then looking him in the eye. "I'm sorry, Mac."

Mac waves his hand to indicate that there's nothing to apologise for. He sits down beside the fire, and with that, bit by bit, I get Mac's story spoken in Jac's words.

"I was raised in a rural area in the north of the island. Cutting peat on the high ground, fishing in the sea when it was calm enough, milking one cow, raising a few sheep and growing a few spuds and oats – that was the life on every croft in the area – a croft is what we call a *tyddyn*, a smallholding. Church every Sunday, a boat to the mainland maybe twice a year. Selling every lamb to pay the landowner's rent. He lived in a big castle and had evicted most of the people off his land to make it into a place to hunt deer and manage the heather moors for grouse shooting.

"I'm related to an old family of MacDonalds, like many of the islanders on Skye. We're Gaels, we speak Gaelic, sing the old songs on the old instruments, part of the old Celtic civilization of western Europe. Like most of the Macs in Scotland, we lost our land and our rights after a big battle against an English army some hundred and fifty years ago.

"From being a free and independent people, we fell

under the thumb of hard and selfish landowners. Hundreds of thousands were turned out of their homes – hundreds of thousands of young people emigrated to Canada and New Zealand and to all parts of the world. For those who remained, the choice was between tugging your forelock to the landowner or joining the army and going to fight Britain's wars in Africa and Asia. We have an old saying: 'You don't teach a dog with a stick', but that's how were being treated.

"I joined the Scots Fusiliers when war broke out in South Africa between the Boers and the British. The landowner came round the villages on the Isle of Skye, looking to recruit young men to the army. 'Every young man who goes to fight for the British Empire in the Boer War will get a 15-acre smallholding!' That was the big man's big promise.

"So there's me, just like many other lads from Skye, putting my name down on the army register. Yes, I can read and write, you see. As a bairn, I went to a little school in the north of Skye. There I learned to recite 'Mairrie had a little lamb' and sing 'God Save the Queen' and count 'one, two, three' and write the calendar in English – like you. I've already told you about the fox's head the children got on their head if they were caught speaking Gaelic, and the caning for the one wearing it at the end of the afternoon.

"At military camp I learned marching and shooting rifles then, and then a ship from Southampton to South Africa. On the ship there was also a company of Welch

Fusiliers and a young red-headed man among the Welsh caught my attention. He looked like a real Celt, very similar to the red-headed folk of the far northern isles. We spent a lot of time together and Dei Coch became a close friend to me. He talked about Llangernyw and I told him about Skye. We were amazed how similar our lives had been in two places so far apart.

"After reaching Durban, we were pitched unceremoniously into war. Marching, fighting, marching, fighting. Sometimes just us, sometimes with the Welsh at our sides. That was when we learned who was the enemy. We had no idea who this 'Boer' was before then. They're Dutch people who had emigrated to South Africa, Europeans like us, and the meaning of the word '*boer*' in their language is 'farmer'. We had left farms and crofts in Scotland to go and chase farmers off their land in South Africa.

"The reason for the war was because gold and diamonds had been discovered in the Boer's lands in the Transvaal and the Orange Free State. The British Empire had decided it wanted the land – and the treasure – and so it was necessary to drive the farmers out of there. We were part of a huge army – half a million professional soldiers under the leadership of Kitchener against 50,000 farmers.

"But the Boers knew the land. We weren't two armies facing each other on open ground. The Boers would attack quickly, often at night, and hide out in the mountains and the wilderness. They were too fast and too cunning for us. Many soldiers were being killed and many more were lost to the diseases of that hot continent. We were fighting for money; the Boers were fighting for their families' survival.

"As things weren't going well for us, Kitchener lost his head. As the fighting force of the Boers were living as fugitives out in the wilds, there was no one left to defend their homes. So we had orders to burn the farms and kill their animals, and burn their main towns. In September 1901, the Welsh troops and our boys were sent to the town of Reitz to kill everyone and burn it down. Then the farms. We of all people – lads from crofts with only one cow and a handful of sheep – killing the lovely cattle of the Boer valleys. And then, worse than that, rounding up the wives and children that had escaped the killings into big concentration camps to be starved to death, and all to break the spirit of the Boars.

"I'm telling you, that made them all the more determined to win. In the end, it was we who were broken. It was high time for us to leave the barbarism and that's what happened in the end.

"Ship back to Southampton, leave the army and go back to little villages on the Isle of Skye to look for the crofts we'd been promised. But it was a pack of lies. The landowner had changed his mind as so many of us had come back alive!

"I learned to be a gamekeeper on one of the big estates in Scotland but the place was full of bitter memories, so I had to leave. I contacted Dei Coch and I heard about the estate here in Llangernyw, and here I am.

"But that doesn't properly explain what happened this morning. I thought I'd got rid of the awful nightmares about that disgraceful war. But when the glasshouse door closed on me today and when I heard the click of the lock, I was back in Reitz. Some Sassenach officer had told a gang of us to herd small groups of old women, mothers and children into a wooden building with a lot of windows, behind the high street. It may well have been a school. I was in one of the rooms trying to quieten these poor people when I heard the outer door being locked. In no time there was the smell of smoke coming into the room. They'd been ordered to burn the place with the people inside.

"The flames had started to take hold when I ran back to the door. I had to go through the smoke and stand by a wall that was on fire to break the glass of the door with the butt of my rifle and escape. I was the last to come out of that building in Reitz alive. But my clothes were on fire and I lost half the skin of my face. That's why I look like I do. And that's why my stammer comes back sometimes – I've had it since I had the fox's head in the infants' school on the Isle of Skye when I was a boy."

After Jac had come to the end of Mac's story, the four of us stared at the fire for a few minutes. Then he said this, and Jac translated for us: "I wasn't angry with Bob this morning, but angry with the Sassenachs – the landowner, Kitchener, the fox's head ... and I apologise for shouting."

"Is it any wonder, Mac *bach*?" Nain Bicycle says. "Is it any wonder that you feel like shouting sometimes."

Mac stands up and runs his hand down his red beard.

"*Ti*," he says to me. "*Ti* learn Sassenach. Me learn Cymrrraeg. *Iawn*?"

"*Iawn*, Mac, alright, I will," I say, accepting his hand and shaking it with a smile.

He said something else to Jac, who smiles broadly as he translates for us: "You and your brother may come to the gardens at the Plas to earn your shillings and to teach me Welsh – but tell that other brother of yours to go and earn his shillings somewhere else, somewhere far away from my pheasants!"

With a roaring laugh, Mac ducks his head and goes out through the door.

* * *

That Sunday evening, Dad feels strong enough to go for a little walk along the ridge road alongside the upland meadows. He has a hazel stick in his right hand and his hip moves rather jerkily.

"I feel old and lame," he says to us as we walk carefully along. "It feels like only yesterday when I would bound across these meadows like a hare!"

But slowly, slowly we reach that spot with, to me, the best view in the world. Spring is painting the hedgerows and the willow and hazel with delicate colours, and the mountains look mighty against the setting sun.

Before turning back, we stand in silence, marvelling at the scene before us. Then Dad says: "You know, Bob, I feel myself getting stronger from seeing this land here. I really do. I'll get better now the spring is really here, I'm sure of it."

Little did we know that it was going to take more than a few weeks of spring for Dad to be well again. There were over two more years of living on the parish facing us as a family.

Part 3

Llangernyw, September 1907

Chapter 1

"Hey, Bob, have you got a story for us this afternoon?" Beryl is her name. She's just started at Ysgol y Llan a month ago and I cannot help but think of how I felt when I was going through the same thing three years ago.

It's Friday afternoon. After the bell rings and we are released from our lessons for the last time that week, a gang of us have started to get together in a square of land on the other side of the footbridge. By now we have a name for this spot – 'Footbridge Yard'. By now I'm one of the oldest in the school, ten years old and in the class that's preparing to go the County School in Llanrwst next year.

If the weather's fine, we gather there for half an hour or so before going home for our tea. I've read about children meeting like this in other parts of Wales and today I have something I'm bursting to share with the rest of the gang.

"Welshies! No yoose! No yoose at all!" That's Harri, and two or three of his cronies going past and name-calling from the far end of the footpath.

"Get lost, you idiot, before we chuck you in the Collen," Aled shouts after him.

"No story this afternoon, Beryl," I say, "but I've got a piece of history to tell you. History that's happening today, it is, so it's live history. What's exciting is that we can be part of it. In other words – we can create history."

Everyone's listening now. About twenty of us have been meeting like this in the Footpath Yard, and since school re-stared after the summer holidays, we're an even bigger group, as about half a dozen new children have joined us.

"I was reading in a back copy of *Cymru'r Plant* about a children's society that's started in Wales. It's called Urdd y Delyn. Branches are being set up in several areas of Wales and in towns in England like Liverpool and Manchester where lots of children speak Welsh."

"What does 'Urdd' mean?" Beryl asks.

"It's another word for a society," I reply. "But it's an organisation with a particular aim, and the Urdd y Delyn has four aims."

"What are they, Bob," asks Eifiona.

"First, speak Welsh with each other and learn to read and write Welsh properly."

"Well, we do that, don't we," Aled says. "Everyone except Harri."

"There's always something new to learn and there are more things to read in Welsh every day," I say. "Some of us have Welsh books at home, but do we share them? No. We need a place to bring our books and magazines together and to lend them to each other."

"A sort of Welsh library, you mean, Bob?" Gwyneth asks. "Oh! That would be good! I'd love to go there and help younger children to read. But where?"

"We'll come back to that. The second Urdd y Delyn thing is to learn the history of Wales. Know what happened yesterday, think about what we should do today and aim for a tomorrow that's better than what we have at the moment."

"Mam sometimes tells me stories of how it was when she was a little girl," Beryl says. "She calls it 'ancient history'; stories like that do you mean, Bob?"

"History includes that but it also takes us back to our grandparents' time, and much further back than that," I say then. "The stories of Welsh heroes, the history of castles and churches, the history of farming and fishing – our history of our own country."

"Oh, the kind of stories you tell, yes, Bob?" asks Gwyn, who's about a year younger than me.

"Stories like the ones in *Cymru'r Plant*," I say. "And also stories about Llangernyw – this place has plenty to tell us. And the third aim of Urdd y Delyn is that children today learn to play the harp and sing old Welsh tunes."

"Oh! That's a good one!" says Eifiona, her eyes bright. "We'll have Welsh songs, then?"

"My *nain* can play the harp," says Beryl, smiling broadly.

Beryl's *nain* is Sioned Tŷ Du. She lives on a farm on the bank of the river Collen, below our Footbridge Yard. When there's a wedding in the church Sioned plays her harp in the lychgate. She also takes it to the Stag inn sometimes, when there's a harvest supper or at Christmas time, and they say that on those nights she gets a good party going until the small hours.

"And the fourth aim, the last one," I say, "is to live as Welsh people. Learn the best things, to preserve them but also to enjoy them and make them part of our lives."

"I definitely want to see a branch of Urdd y Delyn in our village," Aled says.

"And me!" agrees Eifiona. "Can't we have one?"

"It's easy enough," I say. "We don't need to ask permission. We just need to do it ourselves. From what I've read, it's the children who keep the branches alive. They call the meetings. Every meeting starts with singing a song in Welsh, then someone reads a good piece they've come across since the last meeting. They sometimes have local history walks, or tell stories or hold competitions."

"*Steddfod!*" Eifiona shouts. "We could have an *eisteddfod!*"

"I'm going to ask Nain to give me harp lessons," says Beryl.

"Dad's good at writing verses," Gwyn says. Gwyn is the son of Cledwyn the carpenter. "He could teach us to make up rhymes."

"But where?" asks Gwyneth. "Where will this happen?"

"What's wrong with starting right here, right now?" I suggest. "The Footbridge Yard after school on a Friday's as good a place as any, wouldn't you say?"

"Yes, so long as it's fine," says Aled.

"We'll go with it for the time being," I say. "We can go into the lychgate if it's raining. What will be our first meeting?"

"Singing – we have to sing together," says Eifiona.

"What song does everyone know?" asks Gwyneth.

"What about starting with 'Hen Wlad fy Nhadau'?" Eifiona suggests. "It'd be no bad thing to start with what the English call 'Land of My Fathers' from time to time, would it?"

"Alright, we'll do that," I say. I'm looking at some of the older schoolchildren. "Geraint, will you pick out a reading for next week? And what shall we do after that?"

"I know! I'll ask Nain to come here with her harp!" offers Beryl.

"Next week, I'll note the name of everyone who comes to the first meeting and I'll send the list to *Cymru'r Plant*," I say. Urdd y Delyn has almost two thousand members already, so although we're only a little group, we're part of something big already."

"Two thousand! Two thousand of the children of Wales!" says Aled. There's a growing excitement spreading through the group. In that excitement, I sense a new-found pride.

"Seeing as we didn't have a song to start with," Eifiona says, "can we finish with one today before going home for tea?"

"What shall we have, Eifiona?"

"Well, everyone knows at least the chorus of 'Hen Wlad fy Nhadau' by heart, especially as the crowds have started singing it at rugby internationals now. Shall we have that?" Eifiona sings the first verse:

Mae hen wlad fy nhadau yn annwyl i mi,
Gwlad beirdd a chantorion, enwogion o fri;

Ei gwrol ryfelwyr, gwladgarwyr tra mâd,
Dros ryddid gollasant eu gwaed.

Then everyone joins in the chorus:

Gwlad, gwlad, pleidiol wyf i'm gwlad.
Tra môr yn fur i'r bur hoff bau,
O bydded i'r heniaith barhau.

At the end of the chorus Eifiona points at Aled, who has a good voice, and he sings:

Hen Gymru fynyddig, paradwys y bardd,
Pob dyffryn, pob clogwyn, i'm golwg sydd hardd;
Trwy deimlad gwladgarol, mor swynol yw si
Ei nentydd, afonydd, i fi.

Then the chorus from everyone again:

Gwlad, gwlad, pleidiol wyf i'm gwlad.
Tra môr yn fur i'r bur hoff bau,
O bydded i'r heniaith barhau.

Aled points at Gwyneth and she concludes with:

Os treisiodd y gelyn fy ngwlad dan ei droed,
Mae heniaith y Cymry mor fyw ag erioed,
Ni luddiwyd yr awen gan erchyll law brad,
Na thelyn berseiniol fy ngwlad.

Eifiona leads us in singing the chorus, and as she's drawing it to a close, Gwyn conducts the air and leads us into an encore chorus:

Gwlad, gwlad, pleidiol wyf i'm gwlad.
Tra môr yn fur i'r bur hoff bau,
O bydded i'r heniaith barhau.

As we leave the Footbridge Yard, some are still humming and singing the chorus quietly. As I walk home alone, now that Owie is in his second year at the County School, I can't help but feel that September – the last month of summer – is the start of a new term in Llangernyw.

Chapter 2

"*Ydi Dad ti yn iawn ar ôl gweithio?*" I've bumped into Mac in Coed Twlc. This time of year I walk home on the path through the woods so I can collect hazel nuts on the way.

"My dad's very well, thank you, Mac," I reply in Welsh to his enquiry about Dad's health. "The pain in his back hasn't returned." After three years of being unable to work, Dad is pleased to be working as a farm hand and earning a wage once again.

"*Da iawn, was.* Very good," Mac says. It's nice to be able to chat in Welsh with him like this, and he's taught me a lot of English words too.

Back at home, Jac's in the yard. The college term in Bangor hasn't stared yet but he'll be off soon to his second year there. I tell him that we've set up a branch of Urdd y Delyn and we'll be holding different activities. He's delighted with the news.

"That's exactly what's needed in this village," he says. "In college, there are students from all parts of Wales. By now lots of schools have changed to include Welsh as part of their education. Llangernyw is trailing far behind."

"How come some schools can study Welsh and we aren't even allowed to speak Welsh?"

"The fault lies with the headmaster and the church having too much power," he says. "But things are changing. Wales has its own Education Department in the Board of Education now."

"Can't this Education Department force things to change in Ysgol y Llan?"

"They've just appointed the first Chief Inspector of Schools for Wales," Jac says, excitement in his voice. "It's O. M. Edwards – Owen Edwards, who's written so many textbooks in Welsh already and also, of course, edits *Cymru'r Plant* every month."

"Does that mean he won't be working on the magazine any more?" There must have been a note of deep concern in my voice because Jac is quick to reassure me.

"Oh, no, *Cymru'r Plant* and all his writing is more important than ever, judging by what Owen Edwards has said.

"Oh, thank goodness for that."

"In the paper, I read that Owen Edwards promises to change things and those changes will happen at once. He won't see another generation of children from Wales having their minds stunted and distorted, he says, because of some 'unpatriotic, inflexible, ignorant teachers' – those were his very words!"

"And that's a perfect description of some of the teachers in this village!"

"But, thankfully, there are others who are totally different," Jac says. "As part of my course, I've met Llew Tegid, former headmaster of Ysgol y Garth, who's raising money to develop the university He's a poet and a man of letters and he's been to parliament in London on behalf of the best teachers in the county, where he gained the right to use more Welsh in schools in Wales . He's part of a movement that's campaigning to reach three million Welsh speakers in Wales! When I and some of the other students met him, he reached into his bag and pulled out a wooden Welsh Not. It was the largest I'd ever seen – it was huge! Do you know where it had come from?

"No. Where?"

"Some workmen found it under the floorboards in Ysgol y Garth before he left. As he showed it to us, he said 'There'll be no place for such a disgusting thing as this in Welsh education ever again. We're creating a new university building on the hill here in Bangor and Welsh education is an important part of that. The teachers of the future, who will teach the children of Wales about their history and their language will come from this university.' Those were his words."

"About time too," I say. "It's a pity there isn't a hole in the floor of Llangernyw school too, so we can stuff that old Welsh Not through it and into oblivion for ever."

"Yes," says Jac. "But remember, I hear stories from the other students at college in Bangor. Many of them feel the same way as we do – but they say that things are worse in some areas. The Welsh Not has done its work and half the children speak English with each other, even when they're not in school."

"Half the children!" That's quite a shock to me.

"'You don't know you're born, Jac *bach*!' – that's what Morgan from Tonypandy said to me in Bangor. 'It's more or less too late to get them to change back to Welsh down there, *t'wel*.' This is a problem for the whole of Wales, not just here in Llangernyw."

The following week in school, the Colonel from the Plas appears in the classroom with an important announcement.

"I have decided to make a gift to the school, boys and girls. I will donate a flag pole to the Church of England Llangerniew School, and on every Empire Day and for national celebrations such as a coronation or the birth of a royal child, the national flag will be flown in front of the school."

Then he opens a package and shows us the Union Jack, unfolding it right out until it is fully open in front of us.

"Hurrah!" shout Mr and Mrs Barnwell, clapping their hands and showing that we should follow suit.

The flag is put up on the classroom wall beside the map of the world that shows the British Empire lands coloured pink. By now, the pink covers about a quarter of all the land in the world.

The following day a gang of workmen arrives to erect the flagpole. The bell rings when everything is ready and we form into lines in front of the pole. The Colonel comes out of the school with the flag over his arm. In a dignified manner, and terribly, terribly importantly, he ties the flag to the flagpole's halyard and raises it aloft above the school.

"Now salute the Empire flag!" shouts Mr Barnwell.

We all hold our hands to our foreheads, as we've been taught.

"Now march back to the school," shouts the Colonel, clicking his fingers to keep marching time. Backs and arms straight, chests out, heads up.

"This village has sent men to the British Army to serve in the wars of the Empire in the past," the Colonel tells us, once we're back at our desks. "It will be proud to so in the future when you, a new generation, will be needed to fill in the ranks in the battles to come so that our Empire may remain strong and powerful. When was the Battle of Waterloo?"

We all recite:

"18th June 1815."

"When was the Charge of the Light Brigade during the Battle of Balaclava?"

"25th October 1854."

"When was the Battle of Rorke's Drift during the Anglo-Zulu War?"

"22nd January 1879."

"Excellent work, Mr Barnwell!"

The following morning, the vicar, Reverend Powell, comes to see us in school. After leading us through prayers, he takes us through the 'Eye-bileef' that ends with:

* * *

"My duty towards my neighbour is to love him as myself ... to do unto all men as I would they should do unto me ... to honour and obey the King ..."

While we're on our feet, he asks us to recite the Ten Commandments, and off we go:

"Thou shalt have no other Gods before me ...
Thou shalt not make unto thee any graven image ...

Thou shalt not take the name of the Lord thy God in vain ...
Remember the Sabbath day ..."

I can't help but think about Sunday school when we reach
this commandment. I look at Miss Elen in front of her pupils.
By now I've left her class in Ysgol y Llan but I'm still in her
class at Sunday school. There, she tells us stories, sings,
teaches us verses from the Bible. She smiles and laughs when
she's Elen Jones. There's no smile on her face when she's
Miss Elen.

*   *   *

On Friday morning, the headmaster combines the two senior
classes and drills us on some of the most important answers
that we have learned in school.

"Let's start with Geography," he says, and fires questions
at us. "Why is the naval port of Gibraltar so important to the
British fleet?"

We all sit up straight at our desks and parrot together:

"It controls the gateway to the Mediterranean Sea."

"What is the name of the capital of British Guiana?"

"Georgetown."

"Who discovered the Victoria Falls on the Zambezi River
in Darkest Africa?"

"David Livingstone in 1855."

"In which colony are habitats of the unique animals
platypus, koala and dingo?"

"Australia."

"How many rubber trees does one plantation worker tap every day in the forests of Malaya?"

"Four hundred and forty."

"What crops are grown in the British territories of Ceylon?"

"Tea."

"Jamaica?"

"Sugar."

"West Africa?"

Cocoa."

"And what do we know about Oporto?"

"Oporto is an important port in Portugal exporting port wine."

After playtime, the headmaster continues to bombard us with questions, this time about history, and English grammar, and he has us recite every times table from two to twelve.

*   *   *

Crossing the footbridge after the last bell on Friday afternoon, we feel as if the week has been a storm, with showers of facts flung at us. There must be some examination or test on the horizon. But now it's Friday afternoon again, and it's lovely to be crossing the footbridge at long last.

"Where have you been?" asks Eifiona, all excited. "Get a move on, there's quite a crowd here and, look – Sioned Tŷ Du has brought her harp!"

It's a beautiful September afternoon and there's a yellowish tinge to the countryside.

"Come along, children," Sioned says. "It's dry enough for you to sit on the walls here in front of the cottages and on the grass here. Look, this is one of the old Welsh harps. Listen to its sound."

With the water of the river Collen behind us, Sioned starts to draw sweet music from the harp's strings. She plays some tunes, teaches us the names for different parts of the harp, tells us about old harpers and sings some verses to the accompaniment of the harp.

"Have you heard of William Owen, Pencraig, children?" Sioned sets the harp aside for a moment and tells us his story. "He was a harper who lived above Betws-y-coed, and he had composed a tune to his wife. But he had to go away to a war in France because the king of England had quarrelled with someone. Years went by, and there was no word of William Owen. Everyone thought he'd been killed. His wife thought she was a widow and in time she decided to marry again. The day before the wedding, a tramp came by and knocked on the door of Pencraig. He'd heard that there was to be a wedding the following day, and he'd come to offer his services as a harper.

"'That's my late husband's harp in the corner over there,' said the widow. 'It would be lovely to hear it at the wedding tomorrow.'

"The tramp went to the harp and started to play a tune. Then the wife recognised it as the tune her husband had dedicated to her.

"'Wil,' she said through her tears. 'You've come back!' And here, I'll play you William Owen Pencraig's tune ..."

Chapter 3

The following Tuesday, I had finished feeding the pigs and had just changed out of my mucky-jobs jacket into my school jacket in the barn when I saw a tall, white-haired man striding along the ridge road from the direction of Wenlli. He was a stranger, yet I'd seen him somewhere before.

I reached the gate out to the road at the same time as he did.

"Good morning," the man greets me. "Are you going in the same direction as me, I wonder? In the direction of the village of Llangernyw?"

"I am," I reply. "And I daren't dawdle either – woe betide us if we're late lining up for school."

"We shall walk together," he says. "And I promise I shan't hold you up. Tell me, what hills are those over to our right?"

"Mynydd Moelogan is the one with heather on its summit," I answer, "and then you've got Ffrith Uchaf, Moel Derwydd in the distance, Bryn Euryn, Moel Goch and then to the far side of the village you see Moel Unben and Tre-pys-llygod."

"That's pretty impressive, my boy," says the stranger. "How old are you now?"

"I'll be eleven early next year," I say, then add my own question to the conversation. "Walking the mountains, are you?"

"No, although I am awfully fond of doing that as well. No, I've come to see what the crop is like in this parish. It's September – it's important that things bear fruit, isn't it?"

"Oh, it's been a perfect season, you know. Dad's a farm hand at Llwyn Du, it's lower down the hill from our house, back where we've come from. It's been an really good summer for the potatoes, he says."

"Excellent," says the visitor.

"Which areas have you been to already, then?"

"I was in the parish of Llanddoged yesterday. I came on the train to Llanrwst, and stayed with friends at Foel Gadeiriau farm last night."

"Oh, I know of them," I say. "Were the potatoes alright in Llanddoged, then?"

"The crop's always good, but it needs more fertiliser."

"There's nothing better than a load of manure, is there?" I say. "We use pig manure in our garden at home. Leave it for a year to rot well and the vegetables we grow are worth seeing. But we had a lot of wind last weekend and the apples have fallen and look like a red and yellow carpet in the little orchard. We'll have to collect them tonight or they'll only be good for feeding the pigs."

"Yes, old *Morys y gwynt* is a rascal," the visitor says.

I respond by reciting the old verse about the wind and rain.

"Morys y gwynt ac Ifan y glaw,
Chwythodd fy nghap i ganol y baw!"

"Good for you for remembering that rhyme. What's your name?"

I tell him my name and say that I'm called different names in different places.

"So 'Roburrt Elees Jowns' in school, is it?" the walker observes. "Do you mind if I call you Bob, as your family and friends do?"

"Not at all, I'd rather you did."

"Tell me, Bob, and you fond of local names and rhymes and so forth?"

"It's Nain Bicycle who fills my head with things like that. You'd just passed her house before you got to ours."

"Oh! The old lady who was outside the house was your grandmother, then? I said to her 'What a lovely sunny morning' and she replied, 'Sun before ten, rain before noon.'"

"Yes, that sounds like Nain Bicycle to me." I reply.

"Can you amuse me with anything else she's taught you?"

"Well, she likes posing silly puzzles."

"Such as?"

"What do you see once every day and twice yearly?"

"I don't know, to be sure."

"The letter 'Y'!"

"Oh, very good. Do you have another?"

"When's a man over his head in debt?"

"Go on, when?"

"When he's wearing a cap he hasn't paid for!"

"Your *nain*'s pretty clever."

"Well, she's clever at remembering. But she gets them all out of *Cymru'r Plant*, you know."

"You don't say! Does she read a children's magazine, then?"

"Well, yes, but she reads it for our benefit, you see. She's been telling me stories from them since I was a very little boy. She gets it every month in Llanrwst fair and she's kept every one since the beginning."

"Well, I never. She's quite the reader, then."

"We've learned to read them too. I'm allowed to borrow them to take home one at a time. But I can't have the next one until I've taken the first one back."

"And what do you enjoy most in them?"

"Welsh history. The poetry and rhymes. And the little funnies. Oh yes, and the world of nature – the items about birds and animals are very interesting."

"Do you remember any of them?"

"Well, the article about the fox was especially good. I see quite a few foxes coming out of these woods. Coed Twlc is the wood we passed at the top; we're by Coed Rhan Hir now. The thing that struck me was the fact that there are just as many foxes living around us now as there ever were, despite all the fox hunting that goes on. The fox is tied up with the land, a natural part of life here. And there's another thing – he's clever. He never kills where he lives. He wanders far to steal his meal. He's more likely to be left in peace then."

"The old fox has made quite an impression on you, I would say."

"It's easy to learn about things that are around us every day, isn't it? I read about magpies and crows in *Cymru'r Plant*, then when I see them on my way to the village, I remember what I've read."

"Do you get these things in Ysgol y Llan too?"

"No, but there are some people in the village that understand nature very well too. This is what Mac told me a while back – 'You have to be brave to catch a wolf but you have to be crafty to catch a fox'. That's a good one, don't you think?"

"And who is Mac?"

"Donald MacDonald – he's a gamekeeper on the Hafodunnos estate. But he's from the Scottish islands."

"And he tells you these things in English?"

"Oh no, his Welsh is pretty good by now. He and Nain Bicycle have become friends too. Nain Bicycle pulls his leg because he wears a smelly old jacket and carries his opened gun over his arm all the time. And d'you know what his reply is? 'A cat that wears gloves never catches a mouse.' Sayings from Scotland, things he's brought with him, I'm sure. But I think they sound good in Welsh too."

By now the church is in view, and I tell the stranger about the old yew tree, and it would be worth his while to go and look at it because Dad says it's more than four thousand years old. Just then I hear the bell calling us to our lines in the school playground.

"Dash it. I'm late," I say. "I'll have to run down this lane, past the chapel or they'll have gone into school and I'll cop it."

Off I go without saying goodbye properly, leaving the gentleman standing in the roadway.

The last line of boys is disappearing in through the school porch as I arrive at the gate into the playground. I run into the classroom out of breath, but I'm too late. Mr Barnwell is looking at me like an eagle.

"School starts at nine, boy. You are late. Punctuality is everything. A mile and a half walk to school is no excuse. David Livingstone walked through the jungles of darkest Africa for six years. Come here, boy."

The headmaster's right hand is reaching towards the shelf of canes on his desk as I walk to the front of the classroom. At that I hear a voice from the porch behind me.

"*Bore da*, Mr Barnwell!"

I see the headmaster stare over my shoulder towards the door, his hand hovering above the cane. I turn to look towards the door, as does everyone else in the school. No one has ever said 'Good morning' in Welsh in this school before.

I recognise the voice, of course. The voice belongs to the white-headed gentleman who had walked alongside me from the ridge road. He goes over to the headmaster's desk, takes a piece of paper from his pocket and gives it to Mr Barnwell.

"I have come here to see the fruits of the school," he says in Welsh, giving me a sidelong half-smile. "If it weren't for Bob Jones guiding me here from the upland road, I would never have made it in time, if at all."

"Go and sit at your desk, boy," Mr Barnwell says to me under his breath.

"You go ahead with taking the register and following your usual routine and I'll take a look at the children's writing books," continues the visitor in Welsh, and it's obvious now that he is the school inspector sent by the Welsh Education Department. It's clear that is the reason we'd been drilled so hard the previous week.

"Where are the Welsh writing books?" enquires the

inspector in Welsh after we've finished our recitation of the Lord's Prayer.

"There are no Welsh lessons in this school," answers the headmaster in English.

"You are gravely handicapping the children," the inspector says. "They will need Welsh to serve Wales and its people."

"English is the language of the world," is Mr Barnwell's reply.

"Let me hear what the children have been learning in Geography," the inspector says in Welsh once more.

"Geography? Right. What are the names of the of the three highest mountains in England?"

We all chant, ending each one on a higher note, "Scafell Pike, Scafell, Helvellyn."

"What is the name the hill you would see, were that window over there low enough to see through?" says my venerable friend, persevering with his enquiries in Welsh.

"That's why the window is that high," says the headmaster sourly. "It's a waste of time looking out on this place."

Eifiona's hand is in the air.

"Tre-pys-llygod, sir," she says in Welsh. "We've heard the story of its name."

"Oh, very good. Did you hear the story here in school?"

"No," Eifiona says, half turning towards me. "From Bob."

"What about Welsh history?" the inspector asks the headmaster.

"Give me the dates of the reign of Queen Victoria ..."

"No, no – I said Welsh history."

"*Ond* Queen Victoria, *roedd fe'n* Queen *ar Cymru hefyd*,"
says Mr Barnwell. Mr Barnwell speaking Welsh! The whole
school is flabbergasted. No one ever knew the headmaster
could say even one word.

"What about the Welsh history books that have been
specially prepared to teach the subject?" enquires the
inspector. "The government has requested that children be
taught from that book. Copies have been sent to every school.
I tried to use simple language to tell the stories in a way that
would appeal to children, and to foster their interest."

"*Oes, oes,*" Mr Barnwell says, walking over to the big,
brown cupboard. "Yes, copies we have here some where."

He rummages in the cupboard for a while and then yells:

"Here are they! Books with the name *Ystraeon o Hanes
Cymru* – I told they were here somewhere," Mr Barnwell
manages in Welsh.

"Distribute them to the two top classes," says the
inspector.

The headmaster tells three of the oldest boys to take the
piles of books and share them out to their classes. The
volume has a shiny red cover and, when I take a peek, a
number of interesting pictures inside. But the books are
brand new – they've never been seen before, let alone used. I
look at the name of the author on the front cover – Owen M.
Edwards, M.A. The tall, white-haired man is the author – and
so he is Owen M. Edwards!

"Turn to page 16," says O. M. Edwards. "We will listen
now to Mr Barnwell the headmaster give you a lesson about

how Gruffudd ap Cynan, king of the Welsh, escaped from gaol in Chester and came back to his own country to fight for its freedom …"

And we hear an amazing story – in Welsh! – from Welsh history that none of us had heard before. After the story has finished, O. M. Edwards turns to the headmaster.

"The headmaster will now write the names of the main characters on the blackboard."

Mr Barnwell starts to write with his chalk, 'G R I F I T …'

"No, no, Mr Barnwell. Gruffudd was the king of Wales, so we spell it in Welsh. Come, children, spell 'Gruffudd' for me, so that Mr Barnwell may correct what is on the blackboard."

All together we spell 'G R U FF U DD' aloud. Mr Barnwell's face is purple by now, and I swear I can see smoke coming out of his ears. But he has no choice but to correct the spelling on the blackboard.

Chapter 4

At the end of that turbulent and pleasurable morning, Aled and I are given the job of collecting the books and carrying them back to the big cupboard. The classes are quiet, writing notes – in Welsh – on the lesson in their exercise books. Around the headmaster's desk O. M. Edwards is lecturing the teachers. I see that they, too, are getting a lesson.

There is a space to place the books at the front of the middle shelf of the cupboard. That would be an obvious and sensible place to store them, I think to myself, hoping that they'll be used again soon. As I hold the cupboard door for Aled to put his pile inside, I notice a piece of wood hanging by a string on the back of the door. The Welsh Not! There was a large one with the letters 'W.N.' on it and a small one with a pointed end. I nudge Aled and nod towards them. We both remember having them round our necks.

In a flash, without thinking, I lift the larger one off the nail on the back of the door and stuff it into a deep pocket in my trousers.

Then Aled, using me as cover, swipes the other one and puts it in his trouser pocket.

"Pont Faen, after school today," he whispers in my ear.

*   *   *

When the time comes for Owen Edwards to take his leave of

the school, he leaves behind suitably chastised teachers who are quiet for the rest of the afternoon. On the stroke of the last bell, Aled and I race for the door and across the playground, hoping that no one will notice our bulging pockets. Over the footbridge, and rather than following the lane to the main road, we turn left and make for Tŷ Du's meadows beside the river, over another footbridge and onto the lower road. Leaning on the parapet of Pont Faen, and with our backs to the school and the rest of the village, we look down at the water of the river Elwy flowing away from the bridge, between the meadows, on its way to the coast and the open sea.

I turn to Aled. "Do you think there's enough flow in the river? I don't want the wood to get stuck on some rock or on a branch and have someone bring it back to the school!"

"What about cutting the string off?" suggests Aled. "It'll be less likely to catch against the bank then."

"Good idea."

Using the edge of the stone parapet, I rub the string back and forth until it frays apart. I pull it free and toss it into the river. I feel that I need to say something, as it's the funeral of the Welsh Not.

"Telling tales and finger pointing,
And being caned for the whole lot:
Float far away in river water –
I'm free at last of the Welsh Not!"

And I throw the piece of wood into the middle of the river Elwy.

We are both completely silent for two or three minutes as we watch it float further into the distance and then disappear round a bend in the river.

"It's gone!" Aled says.

"They're all going," I say. "Jac says that there's a teacher in Bangor who had stuffed the one in that school down between the floorboards, out of sight for ever."

Aled pulls the smaller piece of wood out of his pocket by its string. He looks at it for a long time.

"You know what, Bob? I think I might keep this. It's an ugly thing and what it represents is even more ugly. But you know what that Owen Edwards said about history – that there are the remains of history around us wherever we look in Wales."

"Yes, I know. The history here is in the caves, in the castles, in the church and even in our language. Every place name is full of history, isn't it?"

"Yes – but there's history in this awful piece of wood too, isn't there?"

"I'm sure you're right. So long as it's part of history from now on, it can't happen to anyone else ever again, can it?"

"So that it can't happen again, we must keep this history known too. People in the future must know what happened in the past. I'm going to keep it, Bob."

"What are you going to do with it?"

"Not get caught with it while I'm in Ysgol y Llan, for one thing!" laughs Aled. "You never know, maybe there'll be a collection of old things in this village some day. It can be shown in a place like that, and its story can be told to children of the future."

"We need to know our history, Aled," I say. "Owen Edwards always emphasises that."

*   *   *

On a Friday afternoon about a month later, the Footbridge Yard is full to overflowing after the school bell rings. We start the meeting by singing 'Y Mochyn Du', then Gwyn reads from a collection of old lullabies from O. M. Edwards' book.

"And now, we can start our *'steddfod*," I say. "We can only hope the weather will hold. There are black clouds over the school."

Sioned Tŷ Du is to judge singing an old Welsh song, and that's how we start – two age groups with Eifiona conducting one and Beryl the other.

Mrs Minister judges the recitation and the essay competition on the subject of any creature from the natural world. I win that with a piece I'd written about the mountains of Eryri in the winter.

"There's an extra prize for the essay," says Mrs Minister after announcing the winner. "I've offered the winning entry to Owen Edwards, and I've just had a letter back from him saying that he'd be pleased to publish it in next month's *Cymru'r Plant*!"

Ben Lloyd the gardener judges the 'item carved with a pocket knife' and then we move on to Dei Coch and Mac judging the 'three stones' competition.

"I'm a stone waller," says Dei Coch, "and I know that every stone has its place in the wall. You can't try and build a wall with large stones only, nor can you with only little stones. Mac says that stones are the same as people ..."

"*Da iawn, Dei Coch!*" shouts Mac, who's standing beside him. "Very good; yes, it's the little people that keep the big ones in their place."

"Every stone has its own shape, size and it's weight," Dei goes on with his deliberation. "You have to respect every stone for what it is. Do you know that there are twenty-four different ways of placing any stone in a wall? See, I can show you with that stone that's loose in the wall over there ..."

"There's no time, Dei Coch!" Mac shouts. "You need to get a move on. The rain's coming."

"One of the competitors has put a long stone on two small ones – 'The Footbridge' is the title. Another has put three stones that fit together one on top of another – 'Snowman'. We have 'Pig's Head' and 'Duck' – can you see them?" Dei Coch has placed the stones along the bank. "But I think this is the best one ¬– a big round stone on the bottom, a less rounded stone on top of it, and a small stone on its end – 'The Kettle'! That's the one that gets the prize."

Aled takes the prize, and with that the rain starts to fall in fat drops.

"There's only 'reading a story' under Nain Bicycle's care, and 'bardic contest' to be refereed by Cledwyn Saer to go," I say. "What shall we do now?"

"Everyone into the hearse shed. I've got the key," says Cledwyn.

Everyone runs back across the footbridge, past the school and up the path to the hearse shed. It's dark and full of churchyard tools, a cart, a wheelbarrow – and the hearse, of course. But it's better than being out in the rain.

Gwyneth takes the prize for 'reading a story'. She'd chosen a good one – the legend of Llys Helig, which is about a land under the sea in Conwy Bay.

"It was worth hearing her act the different characters' voices to keep the audience's attention," says Nain Bicycle. "You should read these children a story more often, Gwyneth!"

"That's what I want to do in a year or two," says Gwyneth. "Be an assistant in the infants and help them learn their letters and get a taste for reading."

"In both languages," says Nain Bicycle, with the emphasis on 'both'.

"Of course," says Gwyneth, and it was great to see a confident smile on her face. I'm sure she'll be great with the 'babies'.

"We'll split you into two teams," says Cledwyn when it's time for the 'bardic contest' to close proceedings. "This side of the shed versus that side – that looks pretty even to me. The first task is words that rhyme with ...HEARSE!"

"*Gwers!*" Aled shouts out from our team.

"Mannerrss!" shouts Mac from the other team.

"One mark each!" decides Cledwyn. "The next word is *LLAN!*"

"*Gwan!*" shouts someone.

"*Hanner pan!*" someone else.

"*O dan!*" is the next offering.

"*O fan i fan!*" then.

"A mark each for everyone. I'm going to set you a task of finishing a verse. I'm sure it's tea time, so this is your line, 'Put the kettle on the fire'. You may work in teams. Shout your verse out when it's ready."

For a while there's nothing to hear but whispering and giggling from both sides of the shed, and then Eifiona recites their verse.

"Put the kettle on the fire,
Set the plates without delay.
Bring the sugar to the table,
It's pancakes for tea today."

"Very good, very good – and so quickly done too," says Cledwyn. "And what about the other team?"

It had come to us at last. Aled reads it out.

"Put the kettle on the fire,
Put the baby on the pot,
Raise the *draig goch* ever higher
And bid farewell to the Welsh Not!"

There's whooping and clapping all round in the hearse shed.

"Be careful you don't wake the dead with your noise!" Cledwyn says, with a wide smile.

"What was that?" one of the littlest boys asks in panic.

"What was what?"

"That thing that went past my head!"

"Oh, and past my ear too! What is it?"

Everyone peers into the darkness of the roof of the hearse shed. Then we all see it passing in front of the light from the door as it circles the shed.

"Bat!" yells Eifiona, running for the door.

"Bat! Bat!" some of the others shriek.

"Watch it doesn't get tangled in your hair!" warns Sioned Tŷ Du.

Outside, I stand in the shelter of a tree with Aled and Beryl.

"I heard the bat's voice," Beryl says. "It was a tiny, quiet voice, but I heard it."

Epilogue

Storiel, Bangor, March 2018

The group has arrived in the upper gallery of the museum and is looking at a collection of items that tell of past times.

"What you can see here is the reason this place in Bangor is called 'Storiel' – it's a mixture of 'story' and 'oriel', or 'gallery'," says Mrs Owen the teacher. "It's a gallery, showing us remains from the past, and behind every one of these remains, there's a story."

The group comes to stand in front of a collection of items that give a picture of education in the county some hundred years or more back.

"Look at the wooden spoon in this display," says Mrs Owen. "If you naturally wrote with your left hand as a child, you would be punished by being made to hold this wooden spoon in your left hand while being forced to write with your right hand!"

"Oh, how cruel!" says one of the pupils.

"Did they want all children to be the same in the old days, Mrs Owen?"

"You see this large piece of wood with a hole in it, and the letters 'W.N.' carved on it?" says the teacher. "This is an example of a wooden Welsh Not that was found under the floor of the old school here in Bangor."

"What was the Welsh Not, Mrs Owen?"

"Before I answer that question," says Mrs Owen, "let me ask

you one or two questions. We'll start with Geography. What is the longest river wholly in Wales? Yes, Glenda?"

"The river Tywi, miss."

"What's the name of the capital of Scotland, where the Scottish Parliament sits now? Colin?"

"Caeredin, miss. Or 'Edinburgh' in English."

"Correct again. *Hanes*. In what year did Wales vote for devolution? Rhys?

"1997."

"Excellent. What do Welsh, Scots Gaelic, Irish Gaelic, Breton, Manx and Cornish have in common? Sara?

"They are Celtic languages, miss."

"Excellent yet again," says Mrs Owen. "In what language do we have our education today?"

"Well, in Welsh, obvs!" shouts out Anwen, without bothering to raise her hand.

"And what is the target for Welsh speakers? Siôn?

"To have a million speakers by 2050 ..."

"Very good, all of you," the teacher says. "But now I want you to imagine a Wales very different from the Wales we know. I'll tell you what went on in the Wales of the Welsh Not ..."

Acknowledgements

My deepest gratitude to

– Vivian Parry Williams, Blaenau Ffestiniog, for sharing his research into the history of the Welsh Not in Penmachno and Cwm Penmachno
– the Denbighshire, Conwy and Gwynedd County Archives for access to the school registers and records of punishments for schools at Llangernyw, Cwm Penmachno and Garth, Bangor
– the Sir Henry Jones Museum, Llangernyw, for giving me the opportunity to see the school's former Welsh Not, and for further testimony about its use
– William Owen, Porthmadog, for confirming the story of 'Jac Two-Trousers'
– the staff of Bangor University Library for showing me copies of *Cymru Fydd* and *Cymru'r Plant*
– G. Arthur Jones, W. J. Gruffydd, the magazine *Cymru* and O.M.E.'s books for information and quotes from the work of O. M. Edwards
– John Dilwyn Williams, for additional information on Welsh Nots in Gwynedd and Gwerfyl Helen, Storiel, Bangor for the picture of Storiel's Welsh Not
– Meinwen Ruddock-Jones, for information about stories of the Welsh Not in the collection of the St Fagans National Museum of History

- Ifor Cae Haidd for his recollections of Owen Jones as headmaster of Ysgol Nebo, Llanrwst
- Dori Jones Yang's novel, *The Secret Voice of Gina Zhang*
- the book *Hanes Bro Cernyw* by Bro Cernyw Community Council, 2001
- the collection of Musée de l'École Rurale en Bretagne, Trégarvan
- Anna George, editor of children's books at Gwasg Carreg Gwalch for her perceptive observations and suggestions, and to the Editorial Department of the Welsh Books Council for tidying up the manuscript.
- Sue Walton, for adapting this Welsh novel into English so skilfully.

A note by the author

Robert Ellis Jones was a pupil at Ysgol y Llan, Llangernyw between 1912 and 1920. In his own words, while he was there, "Ysgol Llangernyw was somewhat behind the times … The Welsh language was totally banned – not only inside the school but in the playground too." By then, the Welsh Not – or Welsh Stick, as it was sometimes called – was not hung round children's necks but children were nevertheless punished for speaking Welsh with "a stroke of the cane on their hand or, more likely, on both hands. And not just a token stroke either, but a proper blow, which really stung." A century ago, therefore, this was still happening in schools in Wales. He is the inspiration for the character of Bob in this novel.

A copy of the Welsh Not in the Lloyd George Museum, Llanystumdwy

Owen M. Edwards, Chief Inspector of Schools for Wales, and a reference to the Welsh Not on the cover of Cymru'r Plant *in 1934*

Punishing children for speaking Welsh crops up frequently old school log books – it was common practice. Lewis Richards was the headmaster of Ysgol Cwm Penmachno in 1871 and this is what he recorded on 4 September:

> "Find great difficulty in getting the children to attempt to speak English. This week I introduced the old system of 'Welsh sticks' which seems to answer the purpose."

The purpose of the education they received, said Robert Ellis Jones, was to turn them into English citizens to play their part in the British Empire. The aim, he said, was "not only to Anglicise our tongues but to Britishise our sensibilities".

The class of Owen Jones (Owie in this novel) when he was headmaster of Ysgol Nebo, Llanrwst, about 1958

Giving space for the Welsh language, to Welsh poetry and rhymes, to local history and legends in Wales, to the history of Wales, and naming mountains in Wales was to oppose this orthodoxy. It wasn't enough just to get rid of the Welsh language – the names of places and any history that made our children different to children in England had to be erased too.

The same thing was happening in many small nations under the thumb of larger states during this period. In Brittany, the children had 'the wooden cow' – a wooden clog or a sea shell – hung round their necks if they were caught speaking Breton. In Breton it was called *ar Simbol*, 'the symbol'. In Scotland, Gaelic-speaking children had to wear a fox's head, as noted in the novel. In America children of its native peoples would have soap put into their mouths if they spoke 'the dirty old language of their forefathers'. This was followed by a caning or a beating at the end of the day.

We can only imagine the effect of this on the children. It was not the done thing in those days to consider children's feelings nor to note their opinion about anything. The child's duty was to learn, parrot-fashion, and not to be a nuisance to the system that governed them. But the memories of some or our grandparents have been recorded – one grandfather in the Llanelli area never spoke a word of Welsh after having the Welsh Not in his elementary school. Others rebelled and were determined to change the orthodoxy. One of those was Owen M. Edwards from Llanuwchllyn and part of his story is in the novel too.

Who knows what mental scars some of the children were left with. I read widely about 'selective mutism' in preparation

The class of Robert Ellis Jones (Bob in this novel) when he was headmaster of Ysgol Cwm Penmachno, 1950

for this story – the term describes a disability characterised by an inability to speak under certain circumstances. It is usually caused by great mental stress and anxiety – the loss of a parent, moving house, starting at new school, being submerged in a new language. It would be easy to believe that this condition would be common in schools that used the Welsh Not and that it would have a serious effect on the children.

I knew Robert Ellis Jones when he lived in Llanrwst, during his retirement. He was a spirited and active man, a natural leader in social evenings and a proud Welshman, of course. He was a skilled composer of *englynion*, had wins at the National Eisteddfod and was well-know throughout Wales as one of the big guns of the Ymryson y Beirdd poetry competition. Seeing him lead a local *ymryson* in 1970 is what made me learn to compose in the traditional strict metre poetic forms called *cynghanedd*. He was my first adjudicator at such competitions when I started to compete myself.

In 1943, just over twenty years after being punished for speaking Welsh at Ysgol Llangernyw – or Llangernyw National School, as it was known then – R. E. Jones (as he was now known) became headmaster of Ysgol Cwm Penmachno. I've read the school's log book kept by him at that time. It is all written in Welsh. One of the first things he instigated was a St David's Day concert, with one of the oldest boys leading and 25 items presented by the children – all in Welsh – ending with everyone singing 'Hen Wlad fy Nhadau'.

This shows a tremendous revolution in the field of education in a very short time! His brothers J. T. Jones (Jac) and Owen Jones ('Owie' in the book, although he was known by the diminutive 'Now' in real life) became headmasters too, and the education they provided was just as caring and Welsh in nature as his. Ifan and his sisters remained to work in the area – their wages were a great help in enabling a poor family to give the three others a college education.

So the bare bones of the story this novel tells are true, but the mutism condition and sub-plots are made up. The stories of the residents of the Plas, the headmaster and the vicar are based on what facts are available, with imagination filling in the blanks. To fit in with historical events, Bob starts school in 1904 (rather than in 1912, as he did in real life) and he does so (once again diverging from the facts) at the age of seven following years of illness.

The story about discovering the wooden Welsh Not in Ysgol y Garth, Bangor, is true. But I can't tell you if the name of the builder was Samson! Elizabeth Jones, widow of Lewis Davies Jones (also know by his bardic name of Llew Tegid) who was headmaster of the school 1875–1902, presented that piece of wood to Bangor Museum in 1937. The Welsh Not is now on display at Storiel in the city. A small Welsh Not has been kept in Llangernyw as well, and it is on display in the Sir Henry Jones Museum in the village.

Novels steeped in history

Exciting and subtle stories based on key historical events

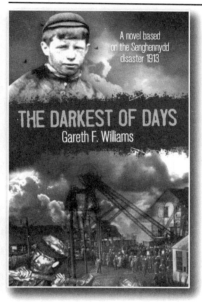

THE DARKEST OF DAYS
Gareth F. Williams

A novel based on the Senghennydd disaster 1913

Gwasg Carreg Gwalch
£5.99

Shortly before 8.30 on the morning of 14 October 1913, 439 men and boys perished in a horrific explosion at Senghennydd coal mine.

John Williams was only eight years old when he and his family came from one of the slate mining villages of the north to live in Senghennydd, in the South Wales valleys. He looked forward to his thirteenth birthday, when he too would commence work in the coal mine. But he was unaware of the black cloud that was heading towards Senghennydd ...

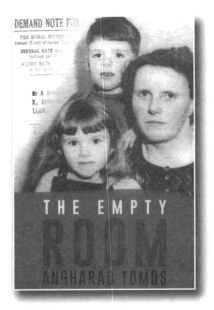

THE EMPTY ROOM
Angharad Tomos

Welsh family's fight for a basic human right 1952-1960

Gwasg Carreg Gwalch
£5.99

Shortlisted for the 2015 Tir na-nOg award in the original Welsh

THE IRON DAM
Myrddin ap Dafydd

A novel full of excitement and bravery about ordinary people battling for their area's future

Gwasg Carreg Gwalch
£5.99

Shortlisted for the 2017 Tir na-nOg award in the original Welsh

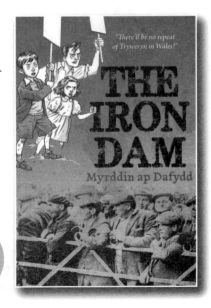

THE MOON IS RED
Myrddin ap Dafydd

*Fire at a Bombing School
in Llŷn in 1936 and
bombs raining down on
the city of Gernika in the
Basque Country during
the Spanish Civil War –
and one family's story
woven through all of this*

Gwasg Carreg Gwalch
£6.99

*Winner
of the 2018
Tir na-nOg award
in the original
Welsh*